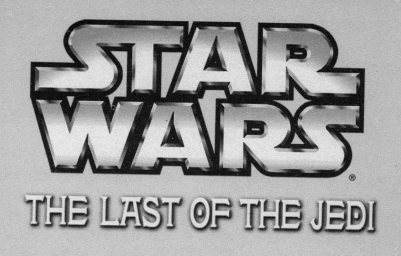

THE DESPERATE MISSION

BY JUDE WATSON

SCHOLASTIC INC.

New York Toronto London Auckland Sydney
Mexico City New Delhi Hong Kong Buenos Aires

www.starwars.com
www.scholastic.com

No part of this publication may be reproduced, stored in a retrieval system, or transmitted in
any form or by any means, electronic, mechanical, photocopying, recording, or otherwise, without
written permission of the publisher. For information regarding permission, write to Scholastic
Inc., Attention: Permissions Department, 557 Broadway, New York, NY 10012.

ISBN 0-439-68134-0

Cover art by John Van Fleet.

12 11 10 9 8 7   7 8 9 10 /0

Printed in the U.S.A.
First printing, May 2005

CHAPTER ONE

Dusk always took him by surprise. On this two-sun world, it started early, one sun dropping first, then the other chasing behind it in a fast slide to the horizon. Harsh sunlight gave way to long shadows that painted the canyon floors with gray.

Another day gone. Another day to come. Each one the same.

Obi-Wan Kenobi ducked his head as he exited his small dwelling on Tatooine. It was time to make the journey over the arid landscape of the Jundland Wastes. Time to lurk above a moisture farm and watch a small baby crawl around the compound. Time to reassure himself that one more day had passed, and Luke Skywalker was well.

He made sure the door was secure. The Sand People were wary of him, but he was careful with security. No one was safe from the savagery of their foraging raids.

His dwelling was small and simple, a hovel, really, carved out of the canyon wall. He had made it comfortable — not because he cared about his comfort, but because it gave him something to do. In those first, raging months, it had soothed him to sweep the drifts of sand from the floors, fashion a heating system, repair a cracked wall that let in breaches of sunlight in the early morning and spewed tiny volcanoes of sand during the fierce, frequent windstorms.

He had found the home by accident, by luck. He had simply begun riding his eopie in a widening circle around the Lars farm until he found someplace close enough to hike to the farm but far enough away that the family would not take much note of him. A transient, looking to start a farm or trade with Jawas had abandoned it, most likely. No doubt he or she had eventually discovered that only the hardiest and luckiest survived on Tatooine.

Owen and Beru Lars knew he was here. Their friendship with him was an uneasy one; they knew he had saved Luke, but Luke's aunt and uncle also knew the threat that he'd brought with him to Tatooine. They were aware that he came by to observe the boy, but it was agreed that they would ignore him, so Luke would learn to ignore him, too. He was grateful for their vigilance, for it meant that they were vigilant against strangers as well.

And who could blame them? Obi-Wan thought, trudging through the sand. Luke had been born in a time of violence and misery. Naturally they would want to protect him. They would not want him to end up in the hands of the Empire — or the Sand People. Or end up like Obi-Wan, a warrior turned into an old man overnight by sorrow and grief.

Was there anything inside him anymore? He wondered this, lying on his sleep couch at night, staring at the rough stone ceiling. How could a being be numb and full of pain at the same time?

There had been so many that he cared about. And now just about everyone he'd loved was dead.

The names and faces would begin in his mind. Qui-Gon. Siri. Tyro Caladian. Mace Windu.

The apprentices — Darra Thel-Tanis. Tru Veld. Their Masters — Ry-Gaul. Soara Antana.

And the Jedi slaughtered in the purge. For it had been just that — a slaughter, shocking, devastating, quick . . . but not quick enough for the victims.

His dearest friends, Bant and Garen. The imperious Jocasta Nu. The gentle Ali Alann and Barriss Offee. The warriors — Shaak Ti, Kit Fisto, Luminara Unduli. And the great Jedi Masters — Ki-Adi-Mundi, Adi Gallia, Plo Koon . . . .

Gone. The word would toll in his head.

Gone.

Gone.

Jedi he'd fought alongside, studied with, laughed with — a roll call of the dead that thumped out a drumbeat of pain with every heartbeat.

And then, as dawn would bring a blush of light to his ceiling, he would turn, as he always did, to the last, worst thing. The thing he could not avoid looking at, the thing that gave him the most awful pain.

The boy he'd raised and loved like a son had become a traitor. A killer. A monster. A convert to the dark side, a testament to Obi-Wan's failure to guide, to protect. The boy, Anakin Skywalker, had died at the hands of the Emperor, and the Sith Lord Darth Vader had been born in his place.

At first, Obi-Wan had thought that Anakin had died in the flames of a volcano on Mustafar. It was months later that he'd realized what had happened, that the Emperor had kept him alive, or, at least, the part he wanted to remain — the hate and the power. Obi-Wan had seen Darth Vader's image on a datarecorder he'd found in an alley of Mos Eisley — it contained a HoloNet report — and he had known at once, with a sense of shock so profound it had made him ill, that Lord Darth Vader had once been Anakin Skywalker.

The only being in the galaxy who could understand the depths of his grief was in exile as well, and he was forbidden to contact him. Yoda was on Dagobah, living in isolation in the middle of a swamp so hidden no one would venture there.

And the spirit who could help him, who had promised to help him — Qui-Gon — could not appear to him. Instead, he had only heard his voice.

You are not ready for the training.

But I am, Master. I have nothing else now.

That is why, my Padawan, you are not ready.

It was hard not to feel impatience, even anger against Qui-Gon. Obi-Wan struggled with this emotion daily. It was his Master who had charged him to take Anakin on as his apprentice. And now it was Qui-Gon who was withholding the knowledge he'd learned from the Ancient Order of the Whills, a training that could bring Obi-Wan some measure of peace. He could learn to be one with the Force but retain his consciousness.

Would that mean he could lose this pain, this grief? Obi-Wan wondered.

Obi-Wan saw the Lars homestead ahead. He stopped for a moment to make sure that Owen was not patrolling the perimeter. It was late, the shadows long, the suns slipping behind the hills. Beru and Owen were always sure to be inside the belowground compound by dusk.

He walked forward, feeling as much a shadow as

the ones that reached out like fingers from the hills. He bent down, flat against the ground, and looked over the rim into the main courtyard below.

The baby had hair full of sunlight, and it glinted, even in this dusky light. He was laughing as he crawled after a ball that Beru rolled away from him. Was it Obi-Wan's imagination, or was the boy able to slow the ball without touching it? If the Force was there — and he knew Luke was Force-sensitive — he did not know if the boy was aware of it. Not yet. Not for a long time, if ever, without training.

Beru rocked backward from her perch on the door-stop, laughing. Usually, she had something cooking about now, and she would disappear inside for a few seconds to check on it. Luke would crawl to the doorway and watch her. He seemed to feel a need to keep her in sight.

Obi-Wan heard Beru's laughter, saw Luke tumbling and laughing with her. He was not even tempted to smile. Seeing Luke gave him satisfaction, but he had left smiles and laughter behind him, part of another life.

Satisfaction was enough for him now. He had promised Padmé that her children would be safe, and he had made it so. Leia was growing up on Alderaan, the adopted daughter of Bail Organa, the kindest and noblest man Obi-Wan knew, and his wife, the Queen. He wished Padmé could know that her children were more than well-cared for — they were loved.

But Padmé — fierce, sad, beautiful Padmé — was dead, too.

Owen Lars emerged from the dwelling. That was Obi-Wan's signal to leave. Darkness was falling fast, and Owen was about to activate the KPR perimeter droids. Obi-Wan lingered for a moment, watching as Beru pretended to chase Luke inside the dwelling. He saw the light spilling out from the doorway and could almost feel the gentle heat, almost smell their food.

He turned his back against it and felt the chill against his face. Without anyone noticing, Obi-Wan Kenobi walked away into the growing darkness.

The next night, Obi-Wan maneuvered through the noisy crowd at the cantina in Mos Eisley. He journeyed on an eopie through secret trails to the spaceport once a month for supplies, and always under the cover of darkness. When he did, he always stopped at the cantina. It was a magnet for the worst of the galaxy — itinerant space pilots, adventurers, criminals. Creatures who greedily supped on gossip and rumor as well as bantha stew and ale. Obi-Wan needed to keep in touch with what was happening in the galaxy. He could withdraw, but he had to stay informed.

The Galactic Senate was still operating, but it served more as a discussion group than a governing body. The Emperor controlled the majority, who simply approved of anything he proposed. Bail Organa was still there, fighting when and how he could. He refused to give the Emperor the satisfaction of seeing him resign. Obi-Wan kept up with these happenings, but he resolved to keep his distance from them. He saw the daily erosion of liberties from afar, as though they had no relation to how he lived his life any longer. If he allowed himself to feel frustration or rage, he was afraid it would overtake him.

He wore his hood low over his face and picked a dark corner. Thanks to a liberal use of bribes, the one-eyed Abyssin bartender watched out for him and made sure he was left alone. Here he was Ben Kenobi, a half-crazy hermit who had no need for companionship. A drink was brought by a scurrying waiter, who set it down and ran off to service a table of traders almost ready to brawl before their multicolored concoctions arrived.

Obi-Wan had chosen his table carefully. He recognized one of the group sitting next to him, a space pilot named Weasy. He was a muscular, hairy Bothan who was known for taking on any cargo, no questions asked. He was also an excellent reporter of information who did not exaggerate. He sat with the other pilots, well into a large pitcher of ale.

Obi-Wan gathered the Force to help him filter out the noise and hone in on what the pilots were saying. He listened for a moment to make sure they were relatively sober. He was used to the boasts and fabrications that made up "news" in this cantina.

"Travel restrictions getting tighter," one of the pilots was saying, his antennae waving in anxiety. "It's getting harder to bribe officials. They're all scared . . . of what, I don't know. Rumors going around of punishments for corruption."

The other pilot snorted. "Bribes aren't going to stop, even in the Empire."

Weasy took a draft from his mug. "Long as it's something they get a piece of, they'll keep looking the other way."

"Look, I'm not complaining," the first pilot said. "The Empire has improved my business. No more space pirates on the run to the Rutan system. But they're clamping down now. Did you hear what happened on Bellassa?"

"Sure, they came in and deposed the governor, stuck in their own guy," the second pilot said. "So what? They've done that on plenty of worlds. They like to tell the governments what to do. They don't like governors who actually govern." He guffawed at his own joke.

"Yeah, well, they had some trouble on Bellassa. Stubborn, those beings are. All the citizens took to the streets," the first pilot said. "There were mass arrests in every city. I think they must have arrested half of Ussa. I'm telling you, this is the start of something big."

"I was caught at the spaceport when it happened," Weasy said. "Everything was shut down because someone escaped from prison, and there was a full-scale alert to catch him."

Obi-Wan put down his drink. There wasn't anything here to interest him. Just the usual gossip. The various crackdowns of the Empire weren't news.

"Just one guy, can you imagine? And they held up transit for a week. I was cooling my heels — wasn't even allowed to leave the Ussa spaceport," Weasy went on.

Obi-Wan stood. The noise of the cantina engulfed him as he allowed the Force to ease.

". . . so I say to myself, who is this Ferus Olin anyway?" Weasy finished.

Ferus Olin.

The name sent a jolt through his body.

Slowly, Obi-Wan sat down again. He tuned out the noise to listen. He wasn't going anywhere tonight. Not until he'd learned all he could about Ferus Olin.

Because at one time Ferus Olin had been trained as a Jedi.

And now, he might be one of the only ones left.

CHAPTER TWO

"Anybody who gets the attention of the Empire has to be brave or crazy," the first pilot said.

"Or dead," the second said, and they all laughed.

"I hear he's both brave and crazy," Weasy said. "But not dead — not yet, anyway. They ordered extra troops because of him, and they'd already imported one of those Imperial battalions. He was running rings around the stormtroopers. Became a legend on Bellassa."

"So what happened to him?"

"Nobody knows. He escaped. They've got a major hunt on for him — want to make him an example for others who might try to rebel. Worth a bounty or two, if you're interested."

"Not me," the first pilot said. "I don't tangle with the Empire. Even to help them. Best to stay clear. Pass me that pitcher, will you? I'm still sober."

"His partner is still in prison," Weasy said. "I

guess they're thinking Ferus Olin will try a rescue, but so far, he's stayed gone." He grunted as he put down his mug. "He'd better stay disappeared. I'm making another run to Ussa tonight. Supplies are low there, and there's credits to be made."

Obi-Wan sipped his drink, trying to make sense of the feelings tangling inside him.

Ferus was alive. Obi-Wan had assumed he was dead.

Ferus had been a Jedi apprentice. It didn't matter that he had left the Order at the age of eighteen and had been a civilian since then. He had been one of them, and he was still alive.

He had kept track of Ferus in the beginning. He'd always thought that after the Clone Wars he would contact him. After they had defeated the Separatists.

That was before he understood how the dark side would not be defeated so quickly.

He knew Ferus had started a business with a partner, Roan Lands. The two had hired themselves out to governments interested in protecting citizens who were whistleblowers — those who exposed wrongdoing in especially vicious corporations. Ferus and Roan found them new identities and kept tabs on them.

Obi-Wan didn't know much more than that. He'd heard that Ferus and Roan became officers in the

Army of the Republic during the Clone Wars, but he'd never had the time to track them down.

After Anakin had turned to the dark side, Obi-Wan had cause to remember Ferus. It had been Ferus who had first warned him about Anakin. Ferus who had sensed that Anakin's great gifts hid great unrest. Ferus who saw Anakin's power — and feared it.

He owed him.

"All I know is, the next time you go to Bellassa, you won't have a problem," the second pilot said. "Ferus Olin will be dead."

Obi-Wan sat, his hands in his lap, his mind busy. He felt feelings working in him that he had not felt for a long time.

In another life, he would not have hesitated. He would have taken off for Bellassa. But everything had changed. He was charged to remain here and watch over Luke. Luke and his sister were the last and best hopes for the galaxy. He must be protected. Obi-Wan had promised Yoda, he had promised Bail Organa, he had promised Padmé on her deathbed that he would watch over him.

Until the time is right, disappear we will, Yoda had said.

But Ferus had a call on him, too.

He could not contact Yoda to ask for advice. Qui-

Gon was not readily available to him. He had to decide. He had to take the responsibility.

Just as I took responsibility for Anakin.

Yes, and look what occurred because of your judgment. . . .

The voices in his head were familiar but no less real. Trusting himself had become difficult.

His duty was to protect Luke. He would stay. And if he came to regret that decision, he would learn to live with it. Just as he'd learned to live with all the others.

Obi-Wan stepped outside and took a breath of the cold air, hoping it would chase away the noise and smoke of the cantina. He looked around for his eopie. Eopies were not known for their intelligence, but this particular beast could manage to slip out of constraints and wander, greedy for the sand lichen growing just beneath the dirt. Gathering his cloak around him, Obi-Wan began to search, berating the eopie in his head. *You'd think if you fed and cared for a beast it would reward you for your loyalty, not take off at the first sign of frost.*

"It is not the eopie you're angry at." The voice was dry, amused. "Here you are, a Jedi Master, and you still haven't learned to correctly identify your feelings."

Qui-Gon's voice seemed to come from the

shadows. Obi-Wan stopped short. He was over-come. It was his Master. Even just the sound of his words recalled in Obi-Wan's mind Qui-Gon's kind, rugged face. And there, the ironic twist of his smile.

"You said I wasn't ready to begin the training. . . ."

"You aren't," Qui-Gon said. "But you do need help."

CHAPTER THREE

"You're here," Obi-Wan said. The words felt thick in his throat. He felt a rush of emotion at hearing Qui-Gon again.

Obi-Wan had ducked into a vacant building across from the cantina. The derelict shelter had no roof, so the stars shone clear above.

"I have always been here," Qui-Gon said. "Being ready is your choice, my Padawan."

"But I *do* choose," Obi-Wan said. "I want to begin the training. I don't understand what you mean."

"When you know why you are not ready, you will be ready," Qui-Gon said.

"Now you sound like Yoda."

"Thank you for that honor," Qui-Gon replied, his voice coming from both the stars and within Obi-Wan's own head. "Now here I am, watching you hunt around for an eopie — which is right behind the cantina, by the way — instead of paying attention to your feelings."

Obi-Wan sighed. He felt old, older than old. Yet it appeared he still had so much to learn.

"The Living Force, my Padawan," Qui-Gon said. "It includes knowing yourself as well as others."

"What are you asking me?"

"Simply this: What are you feeling?"

"Overwhelmed to hear you."

"That's a start."

"Angry at the eopie —"

"Not so. Try again."

"Irritated at your riddles —"

"Good! Now we're getting somewhere."

"Angry at myself," Obi-Wan burst out.

Qui-Gon said nothing. Obi-Wan's heart was so full. He couldn't speak for a moment. Memories flooded him, years of missions, of conversations, of the many ways Qui-Gon had helped and guided him. After his death, Obi-Wan had missed his Master every day of his life.

"Tell me," Qui-Gon said gently.

"I'm angry at my own confusion," Obi-Wan said at last. "I used to make decisions so easily. I knew what course to take, and I took it. If another Jedi was in danger, I went. And now, although my mission is clear, my mind is not. I want to go. But I am charged to remain here. Luke is the new hope for the galaxy, and I must protect that."

"All this is true," Qui-Gon said. "But it's not the only truth. Hope doesn't spring from one root."

"Meaning?"

"If Luke has a destiny, so does Ferus. If the Empire is to be defeated, if balance is to be regained in the Force, resistance will come from many places. All of this together will make the difference."

"You think I should go?"

"It is your choice to make, Obi-Wan. You must follow your feelings. I can only tell you what I see. I can assure you of this — leaving now will not endanger the boy. That much I know. The other is something that you know, too — that if Luke is to rise, he must have something to join."

"So Ferus might be a part of that."

"Speak of what you know about Ferus, not what you can guess."

"He was the most gifted apprentice, second only to Anakin."

"With so many gifts, he is a formidable opponent of the Empire."

"But I would have to leave Luke alone," Obi-Wan said again. It was a duty that Yoda had charged him with, and he knew it was vital.

"You will not be leaving him alone. I will watch over him. He will be safe for a time. There *is* danger for Luke, danger that is close. I can feel it, but I can't see it. I sense that Ferus is the key."

Obi-Wan was startled. "Ferus knows about Luke?"

"No, it is not that easy. I sense a connection . . . though Ferus doesn't know it's there."

Certainty flooded Obi-Wan. Certainty, and relief. All of his feelings had pointed to this. He wanted to help Ferus if he could. "Then I must go."

"At last," Qui-Gon said, "you speak with your heart."

There was so much more he wanted to say, and even more he wanted to ask, but Qui-Gon's presence faded. Obi-Wan was left feeling shaky, but at least he had a direction.

He waited outside in the cold, no longer feeling it. Customers emerged from the cantina, many of them staggering. He was relieved when Weasy came out alone. Even better, he walked with a purposeful stride. He was sober, at least.

Obi-Wan followed. After he had gone a few steps, Weasy sensed someone was behind him and whirled around.

"Who is it?"

Obi-Wan stepped a bit closer. He had deliberately let Weasy know he was being followed; as a Jedi, he could follow him easily without being seen if he wanted.

"Oh, it's you." Weasy still eyed him warily. "Don't believe I ever caught your name, but I see you in the cantina."

"Ben."

"Well, Ben, what can I do for you?"

"Passage to Ussa."

Weasy's eyes narrowed. "Dangerous place, Ussa."

Obi-Wan waited.

"Still, it's no concern of mine, if you've got the credits." Weasy named the price.

Obi-Wan handed him the credits, nearly the last of those brought with him from Coruscant, and Weasy turned and began to walk, not waiting to see if Obi-Wan would follow.

"My transport's at the spaceport. Mind you, I don't like any chatter on the way to Ussa. I don't need to know your life story, or you mine. Got that?"

"I don't think that will be a problem," Obi-Wan said.

Weasy led the way to the landing platform. He waved at a Corellian star yacht. "Climb aboard while I do the preflight check."

Obi-Wan climbed aboard and took his seat. Within minutes Weasy stomped aboard and sat in the pilot seat. The engines hummed to life, and they shot off into the darkness. They left Tatooine's atmosphere, and Weasy set a course for Bellassa.

CHAPTER FOUR

Bellassa had been a thriving world with an elected government when the Clone Wars began. It had sent an army to fight alongside the Jedi against the Separatists. It was an open, peaceful world with many resources, and so, when the Empire was established, it was targeted for domination. Its governor was deposed, and crackdowns on personal liberties began. Journalists were silenced. Dissenters were jailed.

This much Obi-Wan already knew. But it wasn't nearly enough. In the old days, he would have contacted Jocasta Nu at the Temple and asked for details. After admonishing him that he could look up things just as well as she — which, of course, wasn't true in the least — she would put her hands on information in several seconds that could have taken him hours to find.

Obi-Wan felt a lurch of pain deep inside him. *Madame Nu, killed in her beloved library.*

The Jedi Temple in flames.

He pushed the images out of his mind. He could not function if he allowed them to linger. He had to experience the pain, and let them go.

"Here we are." They were the first words Weasy had spoken since they'd left Tatooine. "Security checks before we land. They'll want to know what I had for breakfast. They'll want to know what my *mother* had for breakfast."

After an extensive check, the ship was cleared to land. Weasy dropped into a vacant area near the edge of the spaceport. He activated the landing ramp, then turned to Obi-Wan as he grabbed his ID docs and ship specs. "Passengers check in over there. I have to arrange for docking. Good luck to you."

Obi-Wan nodded. "Thanks for the lift."

"And Ben?"

Obi-Wan turned, already impatient to be gone.

"You owe me a pitcher in Mos Eisley."

Obi-Wan realized that in his own gruff way, Weasy was telling him to be careful. He nodded and stepped out onto the ramp.

It was early morning, and the spaceport on Ussa was already bustling. He checked in with security and then stood for several long moments on the landing platform looking down at the city, trying to orient himself. Even though he had a map on his datapad, it helped to see the ground.

Ussa was a city of circular districts built around seven lakes. The housing and commercial buildings were kept to low height limits. Wide boulevards ran in concentric circles around each lake. It was — had been — a pleasant place to live.

He could see the Commons, a large green park at the very center of the city. It had once been a meeting place, a place of celebration and community. Now a gigantic black structure crowded out most of the grass. Trees and native shrubs had been razed to accommodate it. The Empire had imported an Imperial garrison, a huge prefabricated structure that contained barracks for stormtrooper battalions and a large jail for the overflow of prisoners.

He could feel it rising up from below. The city of Ussa was now a city of fear.

He took the turbolift down to ground level. It was a cool cloudy day that threatened rain. Obi-Wan blended in with the pedestrians, dodging speeders and air taxis as he made his way through the streets. It was strange to be on a populous world again, strange to feel cool air. He had been alone so long. He slowed his pace as he approached the Commons. The presence of stormtroopers was heavy here, as they filed in and out of the garrison. The sight of the soldiers and the building had a chilling effect. When the Clone Wars began, the storm-troopers had stood for the safety of the Republic. Now they were instruments of intimidation.

And it was he who had found them on Kamino. He who had brought them to the attention of the Jedi. They had thought the vast armies of storm-troopers would help them after the Battle of Geonosis. Instead, they had been tricked. Betrayed. Obi-Wan watched the white columns march through the streets, watched how the people shrank before them, and his feelings of guilt and despair washed over him again until his footsteps faltered and his ears rang with the menace of their footsteps.

People tried to avert their gazes from the garri-son but shot sidelong glances of apprehension at it. So many streets fed onto the Commons that they couldn't avoid it, but they stopped speaking as they passed. Even footsteps seemed hushed, and paces quickened as the Bellassans hurried by.

Obi-Wan's steps quickened again along with the rest. His first stop would be at Ferus's old office. It was on a street in the Cloud Lake district, a long walk that would also give him a sense of the layout of the city.

He had seen this before. All the signs were here — the menace in the air, the strange silence. The troops in the streets, the black speeders racing by, filled with uniformed officers. Obi-Wan knew well the techniques of a powerful force tightening its grip on a once peaceful society. But this was worse. It wasn't just fear in the air — it was terror.

It began to rain, a fine mist that made the air shimmer. Cloud Lake was a silver disc ahead as he walked through the streets surrounding it.

Ferus's office was shut, blinds drawn. Outside a small lasersign read OLIN/LANDS. That was all. It was a quiet street, one of the outer bands from the lake, which was visible only as a haze of light in the distance. Shops and a café surrounded Ferus's office door. Small businesses, mostly — an accounting office, a tailor, a store selling ceramic teapots and plates.

The door of the tailor shop was directly opposite. A sign outside read MARIANA'S EXQUISITE DESIGNS AND ALTERATIONS, FOR ALL YOUR TAILORING NEEDS. Obi-Wan crossed the street. On the door, a small, hand-lettered sign read CLOSED, but the door was slightly ajar. He pushed it open and heard a buzzer go off inside.

A plump woman of middle years hurried out from a back room. Her hair was braided in thick plaits around her head, but it had been done hastily, and strands trailed to her shoulders. "I'm sorry, we're closed," she said in a pleasant tone, but clearly, she was busy.

"Sorry to disturb you," Obi-Wan said. "I'm looking for Olin/Lands."

Her smile dimmed. "That business has been shut down."

"The sign is still on the door."

"They did not have a chance to take it down. I'm sorry —"

"Do you know what happened to them? I had an appointment —"

"I'm sorry. I can't help you."

The note of finality in her voice was unmistakable. Obi-Wan bowed his thanks and went out. A short, narrow alley led to the back door of the shop. The back door was closed, but behind a series of garbage bins Obi-Wan could just make out a gravsled wedged against the wall. A young boy lounged on it, kicking his legs. He looked to be about twelve or thirteen, thin and wiry, with a narrow face and a shock of bluish hair.

Obi-Wan strolled up the alley. "Do you work at the tailors?"

The boy gave him a sharp look. "We're closed."

"I heard. But maybe you could help me. I rang the bell at Olin/Lands, but nobody answered."

"So what am I supposed to do?"

With customer service like this, it was a wonder that the shop could survive. "I was wondering if you knew what happened to them."

"No."

"Do you know whether they'll be back —"

"No. Look, I'm about to make a delivery, so —"

"Do you know anyplace else I can get information?"

"No, but I know where you can get a new traveling cloak." The boy gave him an appraising look. "You could use a new one, if you ask me. We've got everything — romex, chaughaine, leathris, even armorweave. But you look like a Ramordian silk kind of guy. You can pull it off."

There was the slightest trace of a snicker on the boy's face. For some odd reason, Obi-Wan was reminded of Anakin as a boy. Anakin had this same way of slyly teasing him while struggling to keep a neutral expression on his face. It had both charmed and irritated him. Every time a memory of Anakin as a boy came to him, a fresh pain startled him, like an electrical charge.

"No, thank you." Obi-Wan turned and walked down the alley, chased by the boy's guffaw, which he had finally allowed to surface.

He crossed the street again and headed for Dorma's Café on the other side of Ferus's door. He ordered the special. He sat at the counter, the only customer in the place. The woman behind the counter had a broad, plain face and a warm smile.

"Not very busy today," Obi-Wan remarked. He

had to work to make his comment sound natural, relaxed. It had been so long since he had to make small talk that it was an effort to remember how to do it.

"Not very busy any day," the woman replied. "That's the way it goes. The neighborhood used to get foot traffic. But nobody wants to walk around the city these days. Businesses closing up every day."

"Must be hard," Obi-Wan said.

The woman pointed with her chin across the street. "Mariana — the tailor shop — she's barely hanging on. Poor dear. Who has the credits for new clothes now except the Imperials?" She bit her lip and glanced toward the door. It wasn't safe to say such things, he knew.

"I noticed the business next door is gone."

She nodded, and he could see the sadness in her eyes. "The poor fellows."

"What happened?" Obi-Wan asked.

He saw the way she closed down. He could almost feel what she thought. A stranger, asking questions. Could be an Imperial spy. This is what happened in the new galaxy. The simplest exchange was complicated by fear, by wariness.

"Ferus Olin was a friend of mine," Obi-Wan said. "I came a long way to see him."

She turned away and started to wipe the

counter. "If you're a friend, then you should already know what happened. And you'd know better than to say that you are one."

The conversation was over. He would not get any information from Ferus's neighbors. Out of loyalty or fear, they were keeping their mouths shut.

At least the meal was good. Obi-Wan bent over, inhaling the aroma, and took another bite. Qui-Gon would advise him to eat. He never believed in wasting an opportunity, even for food. He remembered one of the life lessons of the Masters when he was just a Padawan, something Qui-Gon liked to quote: *When food arrives, eat.* Of course, the saying meant more than that. It was about enjoying what you have in the moment. But Qui-Gon's kindness had always extended to recognizing the hunger of a growing boy.

He was about to compliment the woman on her cooking when they both heard the sound of thudding boots outside. The woman ran to the window.

"A stormtrooper raid," she said, fear in her voice. "Why?"

"They don't need a reason. Go. If I'm empty, they might not come in."

Obi-Wan found himself thrust out the door into the street. The stormtroopers were kicking in the door of an art gallery several doors down. He did not want them to question him. The ID docs Bail had acquired for him were good, but as an out-lander he ran the risk of being detained.

Obi-Wan turned and began to walk away.

"You there! Halt!"

He kept on walking. There was an alley just ahead.

He heard the stormtrooper's quick steps behind him. Obi-Wan made a sharp right into the narrow alley.

He was almost knocked over by a gravsled careening down the alley, the same one that had been standing outside the back door of the tailor shop. Now it was piled with durasteel bins full of clothing. Obi-Wan stumbled backward in time to see the surprised face of the boy, who was piloting the gravsled.

Obi-Wan leaped aboard.

CHAPTER FIVE

"Hey, get off!" The boy tried to push him. He was surprisingly strong.

Obi-Wan held him off with one hand as he crouched and grabbed the controls with the other. He saw the stormtrooper stop and look around. He hadn't seen Obi-Wan yet. The piles of fabric and cartons and the high sides of the gravsled obscured him.

The boy kicked him hard on the shin. Obi-Wan winced. The gravsled lurched, and the stormtrooper looked over and called, "You there! Stop that gravsled!"

Obi-Wan hit the brake and did a reverse spin, heading in the opposite direction. The clumsy gravsled could barely execute the maneuver, but it managed it. One of the things he'd learned from Anakin was that most machines could perform beyond their capacity if you pushed them in the right way. He had seen Anakin do incredible things with a gravsled.

Obi-Wan made a sharp right and careened up an alley.

"What are you doing, you stinking monkey-lizard!" the boy screamed. "I was here first!"

He made a sharp left and pushed the speed past maximum.

"Those are Imperial stormtroopers!" the boy yelled.

Gently, Obi-Wan pushed the boy onto an over-turned bin. "Relax."

A speeder bike roared around the corner behind him, then another. Two stormtroopers. Good. Two was better than one. They'd get in each other's way.

The boy rose, fists clenched, and charged. Summoning the Force, Obi-Wan took one hand off the controls and raised the other. The boy could not move. His eyes were wide.

"You'll get your gravsled back. Just don't move." A gentle Force-push, and he landed back on the bin. This time, the boy stayed there.

The gravsled's controls were hot underneath his hands. They shook. He was pushing the machine well past its limits.

Just hold on a little longer, he told it.

They were in a warehouse district now. Parked along the streets were construction vehicles with hydrolifts, bigger gravsleds than this one, and hauler speeders. One of the stormtroopers flew higher, intending to come down on him from above. The other leaned to the right. They were trying to box him in against the large warehouse to his right.

Timing was everything. And a gravsled wasn't nearly as agile as a speeder bike. But one thing he'd learned about the stormtroopers was that despite their weaponry, their unflagging energy, their relentless need to get the job done, they did not have much imagination. They could not strategize. They could only follow orders.

Moving at top speed now, Obi-Wan had to summon the Force and use it. His vision became sharp. Time slowed down. Ahead he saw a construction crawler mounted on a track that ran up the side of a building. The workers had halted in the middle of a job restoring the stonework on the front wall.

Obi-Wan unclipped his lightsaber and kept it by his side, hidden by his cloak. He had to keep it hidden unless absolutely necessary; if it was discovered that he was a Jedi, he would soon have the whole planet looking for him. He lurched the gravsled higher, knowing he only had a few seconds before the swoops rose to follow. As he passed the crawler, he reached into the cab of the vehicle and slashed at the instrument panel with one clean, accurate strike.

The immense crawler fell with a crash. It flattened the two swoops before they could dodge out of the way.

Obi-Wan zoomed away, free . . . and uneasy.

Obi-Wan pulled the gravsled to a halt on the border street to Bluestone Lake near the Commons. Here there was traffic and pedestrians. They would be less noticeable.

As soon as he stopped the gravsled, the boy rose in indignation. "You could have killed me! And you put stormtroopers on my tail!"

"No, I didn't. No one saw you but the two who just got flattened by the crawler," Obi-Wan said. "You'll be fine."

"I'm not fine!" the boy shouted. "I don't know what you're up to, but count me out." He began to throw bins off the gravsled. "Take it and get out of here!"

"Hey! What are you . . ." Obi-Wan stopped, remembering the boy's cry, *I was here first!* How he was loitering around the alley. He had just assumed the boy worked for Mariana the tailor. The boy had intended him to.

"Hold on," he said, taking a bin from the boy and throwing it back down. "You weren't making a delivery. You were stealing these clothes."

The boy stuck out his chin in a challenge. "You're

one to talk. You stole them from *me*! Well, keep them. See what happens when *you* try to sell them."

Obi-Wan leaned against a stack of bins. "Not very nice of you to take advantage of other people's misfortunes, you know. That tailor is close to going out of business."

He heard himself — that tone of voice that Anakin had always resisted. Obi-Wan waited for Anakin's sharp response . . . then realized it would never come.

Instead, there was this boy, who snorted in disgust. "And now I'm being lectured. This is one swell, full-moon day. What are *you* running from, chief?"

Obi-Wan let a moment go by. He glanced over toward the lake. A vendor stood selling juice and snack foods under a flexible, clear umbrella. He would take his next step from Qui-Gon. Boys were always hungry.

"How about some food?"

The boy snorted again. "Thanks for the invitation, but get lost."

Obi-Wan jumped off the gravsled. He walked over to the vendor and bought two juice packs and a package of sweesonberry rolls.

He could feel the boy still hesitating. He took a large bite of roll. Not bad.

Obi-Wan sat on a bench. He put the other juice pack next to him and pushed it and the remaining sweet roll toward the middle of the bench. He took a sip of juice.

The boy leaped off the gravsled and walked slowly toward him. He perched on the other end of the bench. Then, suddenly, he snatched the roll. He unwrapped it and began to munch.

"So what's your name?" Obi-Wan asked.

"What do you care?"

"Just making conversation."

"So now that you bought me food, I have to be your friend?"

"Well, friendly, at least."

The boy opened the juice pack. "Trever," he said.

"I'm Ben," Obi-Wan said.

"Well, Ben, you look like an outlander to me," Trever said, waving the roll. "So let me give you some advice. If you want a piece of the black market here, you're going to run into problems. We're a tight group. We don't like outsiders."

"Where are your parents?"

"Dead."

"I'm sorry."

"Why? You didn't kill them."

"What happened to them?"

Trever shrugged. "My mother was a captain in the Grand Army of the Republic. She died in the battle of T'olan, in the Wuun system. . . ."

Obi-Wan nodded. "I know it. That was a terrible

battle." It had been early in the wars. Trever must have been about nine years old.

When Trever didn't add any further information, Obi-Wan gently asked, "Your father?"

"He worked for a med clinic — he was a doctor. He died right after the end of the Clone Wars. The Empire sent troops here right away. They wanted to take over the planet's defense system — for our protection, they said." Trever snorted. "So a bunch of Ussans decided to peacefully occupy the defense plant in protest. He was inside when the plant blew up. Boom. Bye, Dad."

Obi-Wan knew the boy's attitude was masking a deep pain — a pain felt by so many throughout the galaxy.

"So who takes care of you?" Obi-Wan asked.

"No one."

"Don't you have an aunt, or uncle —"

"There's nobody, okay?" Trever took another bite of the roll. He didn't express any emotion. Obi-Wan waited while he chewed and swallowed. "I can take care of myself."

Obi-Wan shook his head. He knew every price paid in war, he thought. Every suffering. Every injustice. They were all heartbreaking, but one was worst of all. War made orphans.

"So that's why you learned to steal."

"I move around a lot. The security forces in Ussa

are busy with other things. People get distracted when there's an occupation. And I know places to go, people who'll give me food or a place to sleep. Dorma gives me a meal sometimes. And Ferus used to —"

Trever stopped.

"So you *do* know Ferus Olin," Obi-Wan pointed out.

Trever said nothing.

Obi-Wan continued. "He used to help you, too, didn't he?" Trever remained mute. "Listen, Trever, I need your help. I'm a friend of Ferus Olin. An old friend. I heard he was in trouble. I'm just trying to find him."

The boy chewed, then took a sip of juice. "What's in it for me?"

"Ferus helped you. Don't you want to help him? Don't you want to stop the Empire from destroying your planet?"

"I said, what's in it for me?"

Obi-Wan sighed and pushed over a few credits.

As Trever snatched them up, his dark eyes studied Obi-Wan. "How did you get that crawler to smash down?" he asked.

"Where is Ferus?"

"How did you get me to stop moving like that? Who are you?"

"It doesn't matter. What matters is that I can help Ferus. Have you seen him since he was arrested?"

Trever's face went hard. "He's dead."

"How do you know?"

"Because they want him dead. And they get what they want."

"But you don't know for sure."

"I know for sure that if he wasn't dead, he'd be here. He would never let Roan stay in prison. He would try to rescue him."

Obi-Wan let out a breath. Ferus wasn't dead. Trever didn't know anything for sure.

"I had a brother, too, you know," Trever said suddenly. "Tike. He was in that defense plant, too. He'd been too young to join the Army of the Republic, but he wanted to defend Bellassa. That's why my dad went into the plant. He knew Tike was inside, and he offered to negotiate a deal between the protestors and the Imperials. But once he was inside, they blew up the building."

A remembered feeling rose in Obi-Wan — fury. He knew what the Empire was capable of. They were led by a Sith, and they had cruelly slaughtered the Jedi and caused the death of millions. It hadn't only been stormtroopers who had turned on them. He would have to struggle to subdue his fury, because he knew it would only cloud his mind. He had to turn it into calm action.

He took a breath and looked out at the lake. "Everyone I loved is dead, too, Trever."

Trever balled up his wrapper and his empty juice carton and tossed it into the trash. "Yeah. Well. They crush everyone in the end. The point is to stay alive."

Obi-Wan wanted to tell this boy that merely being alive wasn't enough. Survival was easy. Living with purpose was hard. But the boy was too young to know this.

"I think I can save Ferus. I think he's still alive."

"How do you know?"

"I think I would know if he was dead." Even as Obi-Wan said this, he wondered if it was true. With a dark side so powerful, could the Force still be trusted?

Disbelieving in his own way, Trever snorted.

"Don't you believe in connections between two people?" Obi-Wan asked.

"I believe in my connection to myself. That's about it." Trever eyed him, then seemed to make a decision. "Come here."

He led him back to the gravsled. "You think I'm taking advantage of Mariana? That's a laugh. Her shop is doing just fine. She just doesn't want anyone to know that."

"What do you mean?"

Trever pushed aside the items on top of one of the piles of clothing. Underneath were Imperial uniforms.

"Laundry and mending," the boy said. "For them. For the whole garrison."

"Well," Obi-Wan said. "She has to make a living, doesn't she? And they have to get their clothes cleaned."

"Sure, why not help out the pack of murderers who stole your planet?" Trever's face was flushed. He kicked another bin. "You know what these are? Prison uniforms! They have so many of us in jail they can't keep up with supplies! And there's stacks and stacks of more material in her shop. She hides in there, making prison uniforms for her own people. I think that stinks like a monkey-lizard in a hot sun. She deserves to get robbed! Nobody else in Ussa would cooperate with them — but she did."

Obi-Wan climbed up on the gravsled. He looked down at the uniforms, bright yellow, so prisoners could be easily seen. There were bins and bins of them, and she was stocking material for more? How many Ussans did the Imperials plan to arrest?

His boot hit something metallic, and he bent down. His fingers closed over a small object. It was an Imperial code cylinder — a device that would

41

allow the user to access computer information or gain entry to restricted areas. It must have fallen out of a pocket of one of the uniforms during the wild ride.

He slipped it into his own pocket.

"So what do you say now, chief? Why shouldn't I steal the clothes?" Trever asked him impatiently.

Obi-Wan thought a minute. The code cylinder would only be good for a short period, until the soldier realized he'd lost it. But he would turn his quarters upside-down to find it before reporting it missing. A missing code cylinder would earn a severe penalty.

"Does Mariana know these have been stolen?"

"Nah, she has a routine. I waited for her to leave, then I broke into the shop. She goes to pick up the prison laundry every day at ten."

Obi-Wan checked his chrono. "We have to get the clothes back to the tailor shop," he told Trever. "The garrison can't know that they've been stolen."

"We?" Trever backed away. "Do you want to know the secret of my success? I don't volunteer for anything. Ever."

"You were going to sell these clothes, weren't you? I'll pay you what they would have sold for — if you'll bring them back. Name your price."

Trever named a figure.

Obi-Wan grimaced. "I'll give you half of that. And

I'll add some extra if you can find out anything about Roan Lands."

Something flickered in Trever's eyes.

"You know something," Obi-Wan observed.

Trever shrugged.

Obi-Wan handed him a credit. "I'll give you half now, half later." The boy was turning out to be expensive, but he had a feeling that Trever could tell him things he needed to know.

"My father's old partner — she runs a med clinic. They took Roan Lands there. They nearly killed him, and they want him alive. They brought him there in secret."

An Imperial speeder cruised slowly by, and Obi-Wan and Trever casually turned away. The speeder kept going.

Trever hopped from one foot to the other. "It's not such a good idea to stay in one place for too long in Ussa, you know. We should get moving. We can take the gravsled back now."

"First I need you to drop me off at the med clinic and wait for me."

"Didn't you hear me? I'm not the volunteering type."

Obi-Wan leaped onto the gravsled. "I don't know whether you've noticed, but I only paid you half your fee."

"How do you know I won't take the money, drop you off, and then steal the clothes anyway?"

"I'll take my chances," Obi-Wan said.

"Brave guy."

"And besides," Obi-Wan said, "if you do leave, I'll find you."

CHAPTER SIX

Well, here he was, on a mission. Something he'd never expected to happen again.

Obi-Wan rolled his cloak into a tight ball and tossed it behind a bin. He stepped into a pair of coveralls. Trever drove the battered gravsled well, executing tight turns and negotiating traffic. It was Qui-Gon who had taught Obi-Wan that on a mission, anyone could be helpful, from an elder to a boy like this one.

It felt familiar to be heading toward possible danger. Familiar to keep his gaze moving, checking out the street and airlane traffic, always alert to the need for a possible escape route. The slight elevation in his pulse rate told him he was ready for whatever came.

It was all familiar, and yet everything had changed. He was alone. Once he had thrived in a flourishing network of support, thousands of Jedi all over the galaxy. There was information and help at the Temple when he needed it. Now there was nothing. There was no one. And no planet was looking to the Jedi for help any longer.

He was the last. And this mission would probably be his last, as well.

They cruised past the clinic. Obi-Wan crouched behind the bins. He wouldn't be able to get in using the code cylinder; that was reserved for garrison security.

"You won't get in," Trever said.

"I'll get in."

"Well, if you do — which you won't — find Dr. Amie Antin. She's the one they brought Roan to. Up ahead." Trever pointed to a small gray building up on the left. Two stormtrooper guards stood outside. "Don't let the two fool you. There's security everywhere. On the roof, too. Nobody gets in or out without a check. If you're bringing in laundry, you need to be on the manifest."

"I'll figure it out. Just stop for a few seconds, long enough for me to jump off. Then wait in that alley there. I won't be long."

"You got it."

The gravsled slowed. Hoisting the bundle of laundry on his shoulder, Obi-Wan jumped off. He headed up the stairs without a backward glance.

One stormtrooper stepped forward, blaster rifle at the ready. "State your business."

"Laundry delivery," Obi-Wan said.

"Let me check the manifest."

Obi-Wan waved his hand. "You don't need to check it. The laundry can go on through."

"I don't need to check it. The laundry can go on through." The stormtrooper gestured him forward. Obi-Wan walked past them, keeping the bundle on his shoulder. He sneaked a backward look. Trever had halted in the alley. But when he saw Obi-Wan pass the checkpoint, he waved and zoomed away.

So, he couldn't trust the boy. It wasn't a surprise. He'd find his own way out.

Inside, he hurried past the initial examining rooms where patients sat waiting to be checked in by a med droid who was entering information. He expected that Roan Lands would be held in one of the back rooms.

He passed a harried-looking medic. "Laundry goes that way," the medic said brusquely, pointing to a set of double doors.

Inside was a large utility closet. Obi-Wan put the laundry bundle down, then quickly stepped out of his coveralls and stuffed them into a trash bin. He took a med tunic off the shelf and slipped it on. Then he walked out into the corridor again.

No one stopped him this time as he continued down past a desk full of medics entering information into computers and checking on medicine carts. Someone was delivering food trays. Obi-Wan went unnoticed in the hubbub.

It didn't take him long to find the room where Roan Lands was kept. Two stormtrooper guards stood outside. Obi-Wan strode forward.

"I'm here for a consult on the prisoner," he said. "Requested by Dr. Antin."

"She didn't mention anything."

"She doesn't have to clear medical decisions through you," Obi-Wan said crisply. He started to walk around them, but the stormtrooper held up his rifle. "I need to see your ID docs."

Just then the door opened slightly. A woman in a med tunic stood there. She was of middle years, and beautiful, with a strong face and piercing black eyes. Her white-blond hair was cropped close to her head.

"Who's this?"

"He says you asked for a consult, Dr. Antin," the stormtrooper said.

Obi-Wan put his hand casually at his side, ready to reach for his lightsaber. He stared right at Dr. Antin. Only a moment went by as he felt the sharpness of her gaze on him.

"Yes. Come in, doctor." Dr. Antin held the door open wider.

Obi-Wan walked in. He could see he was in a med room for the sickest patients. There was a med cocoon on one wall, and a variety of instruments. A young man lay on the bed. His green eyes were open but stared blankly up at the ceiling. He didn't move. His dark hair flowed to his shoulders, and he appeared to be powerfully built. He was still dressed in a prison tunic of bright yellow.

"Your diagnosis, doctor?" Her voice was crisp.

"I —"

"Don't bother, I know you're not a doctor, and we might not have much time. Are you from the Eleven?"

Sometimes, if you didn't answer a direct question, you would get the information that you need. Obi-Wan waited.

"Look, I've been over this with Wil Asani. I sympathize with what you're doing, but I can't get involved. Too many patients here depend on me for treatment. I'll give you information, that's all, and not much of that." Dr. Antin sighed and looked at Roan. "You can tell Wil that I don't know what's wrong, and I don't know if he'll survive. They want me to keep him alive, but they won't tell me what was administered. It wasn't Loquasin or Mangoriza — not the usual suspects. I've given him Spectacillin — he's got a slight infection, but that's not what's killing him. And I've done a gas binder on him — that should rid his blood of leftover toxins. But unless I know exactly what was administered, I can't treat him. He's too unstable. I could kill him. I've seen these cases before. The Imperial Prison must be trying out a new drug, something I don't know about. What's obvious to me is that they don't have an antidote either. They just hope I find one. I've done a lot of research on neurotoxins, so I suspect that's what it is."

She placed her hand on Roan's shoulder. "He's just got to hold on. Let's hope for the best."

She looked up at Obi-Wan. "I can walk you out. But don't come back. This is all I can do."

Obi-Wan heard a commotion outside. Dr. Antin frowned. She hurried to a vidscreen and the monitor sprang to life. On the screen was the dismaying sight of stormtroopers pouring through the front door of the clinic. In their midst strode a tall figure, dressed in a maroon robe in a shade so deep it was almost black — as though, Obi-Wan thought, he wanted to appear as close to the Emperor as he could without impersonating him. His hood completely covered his face.

"Malorum," Dr. Antin breathed. "This isn't good."

"Who's he?" Obi-Wan asked.

"One of the Inquisitors — a group set up by the

Emperor himself. He's here as chief of security on the planet. He arrived with a team to train the newly formed Surveillance and Security Corps. They'll be part of the Imperial Security Bureau. The ISB needs a local presence to go after you and your group." She whirled around. "Don't you know this?"

"You could say I'm the new guy," Obi-Wan said.

"It's too late to get out. You have to hide."

Obi-Wan felt something quicken in the air. The Force? It wasn't strong, it was just a flicker, but it had been so long since he'd felt it from another source rather than himself.

He looked back at the monitor. Malorum. That was the source of the Force.

Who are you, Malorum?

"Come on!" Dr. Antin hurried him toward the wall. She pressed a button and opened the med cocoon. They could hear noise in the hallway now, the boots thudding.

"Just don't forget to get me out," Obi-Wan said, as she shut the door of the cocoon on him and locked it.

Obi-Wan had to gather the Force in order to hear what was going on outside the cocoon. The words were muffled, but he could make them out.

"My patient is very ill. I do not allow visitors!"

"I'm hardly a visitor." The voice was soft. "Some advice, doctor. Keep in mind that you have already come to our notice."

"Yes, you are very good at noting things. I am here to serve my patients. Not your rules."

"And would you have patients if we shut down your clinic?"

"You can't do that. Even the Empire doesn't want to shut down hospitals, to have the sick dying in the streets for lack of care."

"I assure you, the Empire does what benefits the galaxy as a whole. It is not logical to consider the rights of the few against the many. We bring freedom to many, but it requires sacrifices. I'm sorry that you don't see that."

"Nice rhetoric. You speak of freedom, but you imprison without charges or trial."

"A necessary adjustment to the law. These are dangerous times."

"You administer illegal drugs for the purposes of torture."

Obi-Wan couldn't believe it. He knew Dr. Antin was afraid; he could feel her fear. Yet she was combating Malorum, refusing to back down.

He felt the rumble of Malorum's anger.

"Enough. You have trespassed on my good nature, Dr. Antin."

He could visualize Dr. Antin's raised eyebrow when she heard "good nature."

"You are on dangerous ground. We know you have ties to the Eleven."

"That is untrue."

"You treated one of them."

"I am here to serve the sick."

"You have a son, isn't that right? Adem, yes?"

Dr. Antin said nothing, but Obi-Wan could feel her fear escalate . . . as well as her anger.

"He is ten, I believe. Walks himself to school — imagine that."

Obi-Wan wanted to open the door of the med cocoon, confront Malorum. But he had a feeling that Dr. Antin could take care of herself.

"That's right," Dr. Antin said. Her voice was quiet, just as soft as Malorum's. "He is a schoolboy, and only cowards threaten children. Is that part of your grand scheme for the galaxy?"

"You are hiding Ferus Olin. You've seen him. We have reports of a suspicious character entering the clinic."

"That was a doctor I called for. Dr. Merkon," Dr. Antin said. "He left."

"We have no record of him leaving."

"Then recheck your records," Dr. Antin snapped.

"You will be hearing from us, Dr. Antin."

Obi-Wan heard the footsteps retreat, and the dark evil in the room followed.

A moment later the cocoon door burst open.

"There's no time to waste," Dr. Antin said. "I have to get you out of here."

"I can get myself out."

"No, they have the place in lockdown. I have a way."

"He threatened your son."

The color had drained from her face. Her lips were almost white as she said, "Yes. That was his mistake. Before, I tried to be neutral. I am no longer."

She glanced at the med couch. "And we must take Roan."

"Take him where?"

"To your safe house, of course. To the Eleven."

Obi-Wan only hoped that Dr. Antin knew the way.

CHAPTER SEVEN

With the help of Obi-Wan, Dr. Antin loaded Roan into the med cocoon. The room opened directly onto a small landing platform, where a medical speeder waited. Dr. Antin deftly removed a panel on the side of the speeder. There was just enough space for Obi-Wan to crouch.

"I had it built during the Clone Wars," she said. "Comes in handy from time to time."

Obi-Wan slid into the space, tucking his legs in.

"Hang on," she warned. "I like to drive fast."

She slid the panel back into place. He felt the engines rev underneath him, and then they shot forward.

Apparently there was a checkpoint, because she slowed a moment later.

"Patient transferring to contagious disease clinic," he heard her say.

"Authorization?"

"Here."

He waited.

"All clear."

The speeder shot forward again. He felt it twist and turn, the engines running fast. After a time, the engines powered down to a purr. Then they stopped.

The panel was lifted off. "Welcome home," Dr. Antin said.

Obi-Wan could see that they were in a small interior holding pen. Several other speeders, most of them battered older models, were scattered around the space.

"I think it's time I told you," he said. "I'm not —"

Suddenly a door burst open, and a Bellassan stood there, blaster rifle in his hands. He was short and compactly built, with graying hair. Obi-Wan tensed, but the man merely frowned at Dr. Antin.

"Amie. I didn't expect you."

"We couldn't warn you. I had to bring him back quickly. The clinic went into lockdown."

The man's silver gaze traveled to Obi-Wan. "Who's he?"

"Isn't he . . . one of you?" For the first time that day, Dr. Antin faltered.

The man held his blaster rifle on Obi-Wan. "I'm afraid not."

Dr. Antin backed away and went to stand beside the man. "I'm sorry, Wil. I just assumed . . ."

"Later." Wil walked a bit closer to Obi-Wan, the blaster rifle still aimed at his head. Obi-Wan could tell by the way he handled the weapon that he was an excellent shot. "Why don't you fill us in?" he said.

"My name is Ben," Obi-Wan said. "I am an old friend of Ferus Olin. I heard about his difficulties and came to help him, if I could."

"Who sent you? Who are you working for?"

"I work alone," Obi-Wan said. "I heard Roan Lands was in the clinic, so I went to see him. I thought he might give me a clue."

"How did you know Roan Lands was in the clinic?" Dr. Antin asked sharply.

"A boy I met on the street told me. His name is Trever."

"Trever Flume?" Dr. Antin looked truly startled. "You saw him? Is he all right?"

"He seems to be able to fend for himself."

"I knew him years ago," she said to Wil. "His family was all killed. His father was a colleague."

Wil still had not lowered the rifle.

"Wil, I must see to Roan," Dr. Antin said. "He's in the med cocoon."

"You brought him here?"

"I can treat him here just as well," she said. "I think the Emperor's forces were planning to take him back to prison. They'd given up on keeping him alive."

"All right." Wil looked at Amie Antin searchingly. "And you? Are you going back?"

"No. I am one of you now. Malorum threatened Adem, and that was the final straw."

"We will protect your son. I will send someone now."

"Thank you."

Wil turned his attention back to Obi-Wan. "I'll call the others. We'll deal with the prisoner."

Prisoner? Obi-Wan thought. That didn't sound good.

He sat in a small room with five men and five women, one of them Dr. Antin. Ten hostile gazes were now trained on him along with one blaster rifle.

"Why did you say you were with the Eleven?" one of them asked.

"I didn't," Obi-Wan said. "I just arrived on your world today. I don't even know what the Eleven is."

"We are a group dedicated to fighting the Empire," Wil said. "Eleven of us began the group, but now we number many more. We —" Wil gestured around the room "— are the core."

"I'm afraid I can't take that distinction," Amie Antin said quietly. "I have joined the Eleven today. I should have joined before."

"We accepted your reasons to stay neutral, Amie," Wil said. "They were good ones." He turned back to Obi-Wan. "We began by operating a shadownet — news that goes out to the rest of Bellassa. We transmit news of what is happening — what is really happening, not what is on the Empire-controlled HoloNet broadcasts. We also do targeted raids. This is no secret. It's why the Empire wants to find us. They've tried to infiltrate us with spies before."

"I told you, I'm not a spy. Just a friend. Is Ferus one of the Eleven?"

"Ferus and Roan began the group," Wil said. "This is well-known, even by the Empire. That's why they were targeted. We don't know how the Empire found out they were in the group, but we know we weren't infiltrated. Until now."

"I don't want to infiltrate you," Obi-Wan said. "I want to help you."

"We can't let you leave here."

"I'm afraid you can't stop me."

Wil pointed his blaster rifle. "Bravado is stupid when one is looking down the barrel of a blaster."

"You will be making a great mistake," Obi-Wan said quietly.

Wil pondered for a moment. "If you truly know Ferus, you know his secret. He shared it with us. You know how he spent his early years."

Obi-Wan hesitated. "Ferus had special gifts. . . ." He saw the others exchange glances. They knew. He would not be telling them anything Ferus had not already confided. Ferus trusted these people. "He was studying to be a Jedi. He lived at the Jedi Temple on Coruscant."

"And you know this because . . ." Wil stopped. "There is only one way you could know it. You are a Jedi."

"If he were really a Jedi he could have disarmed you in two seconds," a dark-haired woman said scornfully. "I don't believe —"

Obi-Wan waved his hand. Wil's blaster flew from his hand into Obi-Wan's. Obi-Wan then tucked the blaster rifle into his utility belt, and sat down again. He would only use his lightsaber if he had to. And he didn't have to yet — that much was immediately clear.

"Oh," the woman said, her eyes wide.

Wil's look of dumbfounded surprise slowly changed to a grin. "Welcome to the Eleven," he said.

"You have trusted me with your secret," Obi-Wan said. "Now I have trusted you with mine."

"We will keep it," Wil said. "But we don't know where Ferus is. I, too, suspect that Roan might know."

"He and Ferus were very close," a woman with crisscrossing blaster holsters across her chest said. "Roan once told me that they had a plan if they were forced to go underground."

"The Empire has made him a priority," Obi-Wan said. "Already today I have seen two raids."

"They've closed down the whole city," Dr. Antin said. "They won't give up."

"We have to find him before the Empire does," someone said. It was a tall man with a grave face who had not spoken before. "They are widening the net. Starting with Ussa and working outward to the countryside. They will cover all of Bellassa if they have to. They want to send a message with Ferus — that rebellion will not be tolerated, that resistance will be overcome. This is much bigger than one planet. This is how the Empire expects to control the galaxy. Bellassa is just a first step among many first steps."

This made sense to Obi-Wan. And now he knew why he had to be here. He wasn't just helping an old friend. He was helping to start the spirit of rebellion. If Ferus was caught, it would send the message throughout the galaxy that all rebels would be captured. But if Ferus could remain free . . . well, then hope would also remain free.

"We had not heard this, Loran," someone murmured. They all exchanged worried glances.

"Ferus is more than a man to the Bellassans. He is a symbol," Wil said.

"And he is our friend," the dark-haired woman

said softly. "We have no leader, we are all equal here, but . . ."

"Yes, Rilla, Ferus was our leader," Wil said, nodding. "He was the one who bound us together."

"I miss his jokes," the woman with the holsters said.

"He made us brave," a man said. "I joined because of him."

Obi-Wan couldn't believe what he was hearing. The Ferus he had known as a boy had been a careful rule-follower. His skills had been excellent, but his style lacked Anakin's brilliance. What had Ferus said to him once? Everyone liked him, but no one was his friend. This sounded like a different Ferus. Ferus a magnetic leader? Ferus with a sense of humor?

Yet it was Ferus who had seen into Anakin's heart. It was Ferus who had stood up to him, to Anakin's Master, and said, *Something is not right here*. It had been a brave move for a Padawan, to challenge a Master about his own apprentice. Perhaps it shouldn't surprise him that Ferus was now capable of this. The seeds for leadership had been there. He just hadn't seen them. . . .

Because he'd always been thinking of Anakin. He had been the Chosen One. And their closeness had blinded him.

"Ferus will return for Roan. He thinks he's still in prison. We must find him and tell him not to return."

"Roan knows where he is," the woman named Rilla said. "I know he does."

Everyone looked at Dr. Antin. She spread her hands. "I'm sorry. The best I can do is keep him stable and hope he fights his way out of it. Neurotoxins are tricky. Antidotes are powerful. I could kill him."

"So if you knew what they gave him, you could save him," Obi-Wan said.

"I think so," she said.

"Amie Antin is one of the top experts in the galaxy in neurotoxins," Wil said. Obi-Wan heard the pride in his voice and saw the way his gaze softened when he looked at her. "If she can't save him, nobody can."

"And I could save others, as well," Dr. Antin said. "These fiends will use anything to get what they want. Our prisons are crowded with political prisoners."

Obi-Wan fingered the Imperial code cylinder in his pocket. "I will get you what you need." He looked up at the ten troubled faces around him. "All I have to do is break into the Imperial garrison."

There was a shocked pause.

"Ah," Rilla said. "Now I *know* you're a friend of Ferus."

CHAPTER EIGHT

Ferus Olin had always promised himself to take a vacation in the fresh mountain air. Now here he was. A mountain cabin, a sky full of stars. He should be thankful. Take the time to breathe, rest, get strong.

Yeah, he'd be thankful, all right. If he weren't about to go stark raving insane.

Ferus stretched out one leg, then the other. The wound was almost healed. The dizziness every time he'd stood had passed. Every day he felt stronger. Dona had brought him medicine — bacta and Polybiotic for his wound, as well as herbs and tonics from this mountain culture. She'd brought him food — too much food. She cooked soups and breads and roasts, and was always trying to tempt him. He'd eaten so much soup his eyeballs were floating. She'd ministered to him with great patience and kindness, and he wanted to repay her care by busting out of here as fast as he could.

Ferus groaned softly as he rose from his sleep couch. If he stayed in one position for any amount of time, his leg stiffened.

The room was spare, with only a chest of drawers and a place to sleep. It was dark, even though it was midday. Dona had made curtains out of armorweave and kept them tightly closed.

Dona didn't believe in ornamentation. She spent her days on the mountains, gathering herbs and hunting, or making the long trip down the mountain to the village for supplies. Ferus couldn't go, couldn't even help her gather wood for the fire, because to step outside could mean death. He had been trapped in this tiny stone cabin for a week now.

It was like being in prison again, without the torture. That is, if you didn't count Dona's constant chatter.

They didn't get much news from Ussa here. They were so isolated that it took days, and the connection to the HoloNet went in and out. There was no shadownet for real news, only the Imperial-controlled information, so he didn't know what was true. As far as he knew, Roan was still in prison. He did not like to think of what was happening to him there. But he was. Every moment.

Ferus waved his hand over a sensor to crack the heavy curtain. He stood by the window that looked down to the valley. He opened it slightly to take a breath of the frosty air. The snow was deep in mid-winter, dimpled and splashed with blue from the light bouncing down from the sky. They were above the treeline here, surrounded by rocks and cliffs. The native *pinir* trees were far below, magnificent specimens with straight trunks extending hundreds of meters into the air, punching the sky with their spiky tops.

Down the mountain was a small collection of dwellings that was barely a village. This used to be a mining town in the old days. When the ore had run out, the people had left. But some had stayed, for some reason Ferus could not fathom. The winters were harsh, the summers brief. The nearest village was an hour away.

A little too much isolation for his taste. He liked cities.

Funny, Ferus mused, staring down at the winter landscape. As a Jedi, he really hadn't known what he'd preferred. Jedi didn't care about choices. They were sent here, or sent there. They took a space-liner or a crowded freighter. They ate fine food or they ate slop. None of it mattered. The only thing that mattered was the mission.

It had taken him months and months as a private citizen to figure out that he could make choices. That he could prefer one thing over another. The city to the country. The color blue to the color red. Every day he made thousands of decisions, and he had to think about every single one of them. In the beginning, it had been exhausting and infuriating. He had hated himself for his hesitations; he used to be so decisive. He had met Roan one morning in a café, when Roan had burst out laughing at Ferus's long consideration of whether he wanted a muffin or a roll. Roan had tossed both on Ferus's tray with such genial good nature that they had taken breakfast together and talked until lunch

The memory of Roan's booming laugh made Ferus's chest feel tight. After leaving the Jedi, he had felt as though the ground was dissolving under his feet. He had wandered from planet to planet. The Jedi had given him enough credits, contacts, and help to start a new life. But those practical things had not helped with the bewilderment he felt.

It was Roan who had saved him. Roan who had shown him what it meant to have a home. When Ferus had come up with the idea for the business, Roan had sold everything he had to finance it. They had become partners as well as friends.

He and Roan had made an agreement as soon as they had pledged to fight the Empire: If one of them was able to escape, he would not return for the other. They had pledged this using the Bellassan method of grasping each other's shoulders and looking into each other's eyes.

Ferus had pledged his honor, and yet he knew he would break that pledge in a heartbeat as soon as he was able. Every day he was stronger. Every day he was one day closer to leaving.

He heard the creak of the door behind him. Instinctively his hand went to his belt. It had been years since he'd left the Jedi, and he could not remove the habit of reaching for a lightsaber that was no longer there.

"What are you doing? You can't stand by the window!" Dona moved forward quickly. She waved one thick, broad hand over a sensor and the armor-weave curtains snapped shut. "I told you, the Imperials are sending seeker droids everywhere. They will send them even here, eventually, or sooner than that." Dona tossed her waist-length gray braid behind her shoulder and moved around the room, smoothing a thermal blanket, moving a water pitcher from here to there, adjusting the tilt of a data screen. She was always moving, usually talking, and driving him crazy.

He was fond of her, though. He owed his life to her. He had made his way here, wounded, half out of his head with pain and exhaustion, and she had taken him in without question. She had hidden him and cared for him and would die for him, if she had to.

She had been his first client. He and Roan had

started the business, and they had barely opened their doors when she'd walked in the door. She'd collected evidence against her employer for three months, as soon as she'd found out he was cutting corners on a vaccine for children that could be tainted. She was ready to take it to the authorities, but she knew she would not only be fired but could possibly be a target of assassination. Ferus and Roan had thought she'd been exaggerating, but they'd taken her on. She had been right. The government of her homeworld had been involved in the coverup as well as the corporation. They tried to discredit her, then they tried to arrest her, and finally, they tried to kill her. Roan and Ferus had spirited her away, found her a new identity, and she had testified against them in a galactic court. She had brought down a government as well as a corporation, and she still had enemies.

Dona was so resourceful that Ferus did not take credit for saving her life. She had taken the mountain cabin they'd found her and transformed it into a fortress. She had planted booby traps and devised her own surveillance techniques. He told her that she would have defeated them without the help of Olin/Lands. But he could not talk her out of her belief that he and Roan had saved her.

He heard the buzz of her conversation as static, then tuned back in. ". . . the trouble with the galaxy now, you can't trust anyone. At least before, you knew who you could trust and who you couldn't, at least most of the time. I should be the last one to say this, of course. I don't trust anybody. But now I *really* don't. So don't stand in front of the window, that's all I ask. Now, would you be wanting anything? I just made a pot of —"

Not more soup, Ferus thought. "No, thanks, Dona," he interrupted quickly, "I —" Ferus reached out to turn on what he thought was a switch for a glow lamp, and suddenly, the floor opened up. He slid down a chute and spilled out onto a stone floor, bumping his head in the process.

He looked up into the gloom. Dona looked down into the passage, squinting at him while he rubbed his head.

"Soup?" she asked.

Roan, I can't wait to tell you about this. Stay alive. Stay alive, so we can laugh again, Ferus begged in his head as he nodded.

CHAPTER NINE

Obi-Wan walked through the narrow streets of the area around Moonstone Lake, the most distant lake on the outskirts of town. Compared to the rest of Ussa, this was a grimy district. The streets were narrow and twined around one another in baffling patterns. The houses huddled together, and the pedestrians walked quickly, their eyes down. Obi-Wan was alert for movement from the shadowy alleys. He had gotten a crash course in how the black market operated from Wil and Rilla.

He kept his left hand free and held a disposable cup with steaming tea in it. He did not drink it, but held it. There were many tea stands in Ussa, and it was easily obtainable. All one had to do, Wil and Rilla assured him, was walk the streets of the Moonstone District holding a cup in the left hand. Sooner or later, he would be approached. It was a system that everyone knew, and so far, the Empire had not been able to crack it. The black market flourished in Ussa, something that infuriated the Imperial forces, Obi-Wan had been told.

"You see," Wil had said, "they can have our government and our press and our factories. But they cannot have our loyalty. Their spies do not work here."

Rilla had nodded. "It is why they hate Ferus so much. No one will betray him, not for all the credits on Bellassa. It gives other planets hope."

It didn't take long for Obi-Wan to make contact. A young woman, her hair tucked under a dark cap, drifted close to him. "What are you looking for?"

"Clothing," he said.

She sighed in disappointment. "I have tech items . . . some functioning datapads, cloud car parts . . ."

"Not today, sorry."

"Then turn left into the next alley and whistle."

Obi-Wan followed her directions. The alley was dark, even though night had not fallen. He whistled softly.

After a moment, there was a rustling sound. A gravsled hummed forward, clothing tumbled in it in an array of colors and fabrics. It looked as if it had already been pawed through. Behind the controls was Trever. When he caught sight of Obi-Wan, the boy shook his head.

"Oh, no. Not you."

"Nice to see you again, too," Obi-Wan said. "I thought we had an agreement that you'd wait for me."

"I get itchy around stormtroopers. I'm funny that way."

"You owe me credits. And my cloak — I hope you haven't sold it. I paid you to wait."

Trever shifted his feet. "Look, I don't have the credits okay? I spent them already. You can take some clothing. I still think you'd look sharp in Ramordian silk. I think I've still got your cloak in here . . ." Trever began to dig through the garments. He came up with Obi-Wan's cloak and tossed it to him. "There. Now we're square, all right?"

"Not yet. I want an Imperial uniform."

"You told me to take them back to Mariana, remember?"

"But you didn't. They could be valuable. You would have kept those for yourself."

Trever groaned. "I knew today was a no-moon day. Come on."

Obi-Wan followed the gravsled over the paving stones of the alley. Trever pushed through a battered metal door and motioned Obi-Wan through. Trever left the gravsled in a small foyer crowded with other battered repulsorlift vehicles, most of them stuffed with objects in various states of deterioration.

There was nowhere to go except through another battered door. Obi-Wan reached out to push it open, but Trever said, "Wait." He stepped forward and waved his hand over a battered, grimy sensor that Obi-Wan had assumed was broken.

In the old days, he would know better than to assume. Was he losing his Jedi awareness? Obi-Wan corrected himself. He had to have the same focus he always had. He could not let the days of isolation, the weeks and months of grief, dull his abilities.

The door clicked, and Trever pushed it open. Inside was one large room, taking up the entire first floor of the warehouse. It was crammed with contraband. Obi-Wan stopped, marveling. Household appliances, droids, computer parts, speeder parts, clothing, office equipment, and even one intact cloud car. The material was divided into separate piles. Men and women took items from various stacks and placed them on carts, or hid smaller items under their cloaks, then headed outside again. Some appeared to be shopping, followed closely by the sellers.

"How do they guard their own items?" Obi-Wan asked.

"Honor among thieves. Come on."

He led Obi-Wan to a far corner, A group of durasteel bins were neatly arranged in rows. He went directly to one in the back. He pulled out an

Imperial uniform of a low-grade officer. But before handing it to Obi-Wan, he hesitated. "Don't tell me what you're going to do with this. And this is the last favor I do for you."

"Last favor. Promise." Obi-Wan took the uniform.

"And don't change into it here," Trever advised. "You'll start a panic. Everyone will think you're here to arrest them." He hesitated for a moment. "Is this about Ferus?"

"I thought you didn't want to know."

"Well, if you do find him, tell him . . ."

Obi-Wan waited. He saw the struggle on the boy's face. He *did* care about Ferus.

"Tell him he stinks like a bantha," Trever said in a rush.

"I'll do that," Obi-Wan promised, and headed for the door.

CHAPTER TEN

Once, long ago, Obi-Wan and Qui-Gon had been walking through a torrential rainstorm. The rain had seemed to hit Obi-Wan in relentless sheets of water. He struggled with every step, while ahead of him his Master's broad back had moved steadily on. Obi-Wan had flinched from the onslaught, wiped the rain from his eyes so he could see, and slipped on the slick stones of the path they were following. Qui-Gon never even flinched.

He had struggled on for kilometers, hoping his Master had not noticed his difficulty. When at last they stopped to rest, Obi-Wan had leaned against the wall of the cave they had found for shelter. Everything was sodden — his cloak and hood, his pack, his boots. He felt he had been carrying stones in his pockets.

He still remembered Qui-Gon looking out at the rain cascading from a metallic sky. "You must own the rain, Obi-Wan. It must be part of you, an extension of you. If you fight it, it will win. Acceptance is the key to all difficulties."

He had been fourteen then. He had learned that lesson, and, like all of Qui-Gon's lessons, it had extended to so many things. Heat, wind, cold — he had learned how to accept them, not fight them.

Now he wore the uniform of an Imperial officer, and he owned it. His face was newly shaven, his expression impassive. He strode through the streets, and did not care that Bellassans shrank when they saw him, that they retreated before him like a toxic wind. For the time he would wear it, he would not shrink from the contact of it on his skin. He would not betray, by a look or a gesture, that he hated every fiber of it, for it represented everything he fought against.

The Imperial code cylinder got him into the front door of the garrison without trouble. That meant the owner had not reported it stolen. Still, he had to work fast. Obi-Wan strode down the hall. He knew the clones were ruthless and unimaginative. The Imperial officers were either brutes or opportunists, or both. They all carried themselves with the arrogant assurance that absolute power gave. They had all been a part of Emperor Palpatine's betrayal of the Jedi . . . but Obi-Wan had to block that out in order to make it through. He could not let anger or sadness seize him. Not now. Not ever.

No one stopped him or gave him a second look. The garrison was busy, with troops filing down the hallways and officers walking briskly, trying not to rush. The Empire had expanded its ranks, and he noted that many of the beings were not clones but crafty opportunists recruited from every corner of the galaxy. The stormtroopers were dressed in riot armor, carrying stun batons and blast shields. Was something afoot? Obi-Wan wasn't sure, but he wanted to be sure to get his information and get out before something happened.

He followed signs in Aurebesh for INTELLIGENCE UNIT/SECURITY and found an empty office. Obi-Wan quickly closed the door and, using the code cylinder, accessed the computer database. He entered the name ROAN LANDS.

Surveillance files popped up. Obi-Wan had been lucky. The cylinder must have belonged to a commander. He had high-level security clearance.

Intelligence breakthrough by paid operative indicates that Lands is a founding member of the Eleven along with Ferus Olin . . . considered dangerous to the goals of the Empire . . .

Paid operative? A spy? Obi-Wan searched, but could find no further mention of the operative. Only a direction to the files of the Inquisitors. When he tried to access them, he was denied. His officer didn't have that high a clearance.

Subject left office, proceeded to Bluestone Lake district. Subject lost after entering large market.

Subject left home, proceeded to Gree Park. Subject lost among hiking trails.

"Good for you, Roan," Obi-Wan murmured. Roan Lands was obviously good at shaking the surveillance he'd known was behind him.

The file was a long one. He flipped through the hologram quickly. It ended with the arrest of Roan and Ferus. They had been surrounded by a full platoon, in the middle of the city, and had given themselves up rather than endanger the surrounding civilians. Obi-Wan could find no mention of charges. But then, the Imperials did not concern themselves with what they thought of as the petty rules of law.

Ah, the med record. Obi-Wan scrolled down to a section titled PERSUASIAN TECHNIQUES. His heart fell. Roan had been exposed to many neurotoxins. He had proven to be extraordinarily strong. Obi-Wan committed the drugs to memory, concentrating on those administered during Roan's last days in prison.

He could hear more footsteps in the hallways and could pick up the buzz of energy outside. He sensed that he wouldn't have much time left, but he owed it to the Eleven to find out as much as he could. As long as he could get inside the database, he had to keep looking.

He exited from Roan's file and browsed through directives to officers, most of them at the highest level of security clearance.

ARREST SWEEPS. *Rotating neighborhoods To Be Determined. Any suspicious characters to be picked up. Targets to include: journalists, writers, artists, weapons experts, former army officers and soldiers* . . .

The title of a directive caught Obi-Wan's eye.

SCEMARIOS FOR BODY DISPOSAL POST ORDER THIRTY-SEVEN.

Obi-Wan felt a chill. He accessed the file.

It is imperative that bodies not be released to family members . . . All HoloNet communication must shut down that morning and comm silence maintained for the next month so COMPNOR can control information outflow. . . . No accounts to be disseminated as they can prove detrimental to Imperial control of surrounding systems. . . . Proof of body disposal documented for Inquisitor Malorum to pass to LDV. . . .

LDV . . . Lord Darth Vader?

Hundreds of bodies. They were planning for the disposal of hundreds of bodies. Obi-Wan frantically searched through the document, looking for clues.

Who would be taken? When? He could find no information. It was as though the order had already been given. . . .

The troops in the hallways. The sense he had of something about to happen. . . .

Suddenly, Obi-Wan felt a surge of the dark side of the Force.

That meant that the full might of security would come crashing down on Obi-Wan's head within seconds.

He shut down the computer bank. Obi-Wan kept the cylinder in his palm and slipped out the door. A troop of officers was marching by, and he joined it. He was lost in a sea of uniforms. As they passed an equipment bin, he dropped the code cylinder in it. No one must know he had been here. No one must know he had seen that file.

He felt that Malorum was close.

A clanging noise came over the speakers. A voice announced, "Order Thirty-Seven has begun. Please report to your stations. Repeat: Order Thirty-Seven has begun."

The hallways were suddenly flooded with stormtroopers. Obi-Wan was swept along in the tide.

He burst out of the garrison. He stayed with the troopers as they marched across the Commons and spilled into the streets, patrols splitting off from each other to cover more ground. A few people stopped to stare while others began to hurry, trying to outwalk the stomping boots.

An elder Bellassan stopped to watch the stormtroopers, concern on his face. To Obi-Wan's shock, a stormtrooper hit him with a stun baton. He fell, writhing, to the ground. The baton was set for a severe shock.

Obi-Wan started forward, but he knew he could not help. A woman stopped to try, and another stormtrooper hit her with the baton. She fell over the paralyzed man.

Holding pens with repulsorlift engines streamed from the garrison, piloted by more troopers. One after another they rumbled through the streets. As the stormtroopers moved through, striking down any pedestrian in their way, the carts picked up the bodies. Screams filled the air.

Rage and helplessness made Obi-Wan shake. There was nothing he could do. Never had he felt so alone. Once he could have done something, could have used his position as a Jedi to interfere, to call for reinforcements. Now he could only watch.

Cries rolled up from the streets, from the buildings, as entire families were taken. Anyone who protested was struck down. Children, elders, women, men.

Were these the bodies the file was talking about? Could the Empire truly do this? Could they assassinate so many for no reason? Or was there a reason? To crush Ferus and anyone like him.

Obi-Wan hurried through the streets. He had tracked an escape route back to the safe house of the Eleven. His uniform gave him cover from the troopers as well as the pedestrians he met. Frightened, they ran from him.

He couldn't wait to remove it. It felt as though it burned his skin.

After finding his Jedi robes where he'd hidden them, he circled around to the back of the safe house. The house had been chosen carefully with an eye for privacy. There were no windows, no doors overlooking the back entrance. Obi-Wan entered the code he'd been given and slipped through the gate. In a moment, Wil had opened the door to the house.

"We've heard the news. Mass arrests."

Obi-Wan took several breaths, trying to compose himself. "They are taking anyone in their way —"

Wil drew him in and closed the door. "I'm happy to see you are safe."

Obi-Wan still felt the drum of the marching feet, saw the anguished faces, the still-twitching bodies being tossed into the holding pens. "You should be worried for yourselves," he said.

A shadow of deep concern was on Wil's face, and Obi-Wan realized it wasn't for him. "What is it?"

"We have heard something. Ferus is in greater danger than we knew."

"What?"

"They haven't released the information that Roan has escaped, first of all. They want Ferus to think he's still being held. And we were contacted by several of the clients of Roan/Lands. Stormtroopers are visiting each of them, searching and in some cases destroying their houses. We can only assume that the Imperials have the secret list of the clients of Olin/Lands. We don't know how. If what we suspect is true — if Ferus is hiding with one of them . . ."

"It will not take them long to find him," Obi-Wan finished.

CHAPTER ELEVEN

Obi-Wan hurried into the interior room where Amie Antin sat with Roan.

"They used a combination of Loquasin and Titroxinate," Obi-Wan said. He repeated the levels to the doctor. "Then, on the last day, they administered Skirtopanol."

"It wasn't a new drug. It was a new combination," Dr. Antin breathed. "That explains his state now. But that combination . . . they must be mad."

"They were desperate," Obi-Wan said.

"This gives me what I need," she said, already crossing to the med kit. "You two, go relax or something. I'll find you if he wakes. I need quiet here."

Obi-Wan trailed after Wil down the hall to the kitchen. The house was soundproof, but they all knew what was going on outside.

Wil put his head in his hands for a moment. "To

go out there would be madness. To stay inside . . . it will drive me mad."

"There is nothing we can do," Obi-Wan said. "We can only wait for more opportune moments."

Wil raised his head. His gray eyes were bleak. "Why now?" he asked softly. "There's been no unrest, no battles. I don't understand the mass arrests."

"Are your people safe?" Obi-Wan asked.

"The core group was all here for a meeting. And we moved our families out of the city long ago. I was able to get Amie's son away, too. He's safe. But there are many others, spread out all over the city. . . . We won't hear word until later." He sat at the table, his hands gripping his blaster. "I don't know where all of this will end."

Obi-Wan didn't know what to say. He had no answers. The galaxy was in the grip of a darkness that was vast and complete. The Sith had triumphed.

"I don't believe they will rule forever," he said finally.

Wil gestured toward some food, but Obi-Wan shook his head. Somehow it seemed wrong to take comfort in a warm kitchen, when outside the doors so much horror was taking place.

"No. And it will take more than we can possibly imagine to defeat them," Wil said. "More than we think we are prepared to do. And yet I hope I'm still here to see it."

Obi-Wan silently agreed. He thought of the children, Luke and Leia, growing up on separate planets. He hoped to see them as adults, committed to the fight. The thought of that lifted some of the helplessness he felt earlier — and also made him aware of the need to return to Luke soon.

Amie Antin appeared in the doorway. "He is awake."

Obi-Wan rose quickly . "That was fast."

"He is very strong. His mind is active, but his body will need time. At least a week before he can stand, I think. The drugs were powerful. Come. I can give you both a minute."

Obi-Wan and Wil followed behind her. When they walked into the room, Roan was struggling to rise.

"Ferus," he said.

"He isn't here," Wil said. "But we know he is safe."

Gently, Amie pushed Roan back against the pillow. "You will be weak for some time. It is better that you stay flat."

Roan obeyed her. His powerful body must have been fragile, for even Amie's gentle touch sent him backward onto the sleep couch. The look he sent toward Obi-Wan brimmed with the strength his body didn't possess. "Who is this?"

"I am a friend of Ferus's from long ago," Obi-Wan said.

"You are a Jedi," Roan guessed.

"I came to help him, if I can."

"I have nothing to tell you."

Obi-Wan pushed a chair over and sat down. "I think you do," he said. "I think you know where he is."

Roan stirred restlessly. "I'll recover soon. If he needs help, I can give it."

"Dr. Antin thinks it will take you a week."

"Dr. Antin is wrong."

"She is an expert on neurotoxins."

"She's not an expert on me, though." Roan's mouth tilted, almost a grin.

"For the record," Amie broke in, "I'm never wrong."

"Are you willing to gamble on Ferus's life?" Obi-Wan asked.

"Roan, we need to know where he is," Wil said. "We have reason to believe that the Imperials are searching for him at the homes of all your old clients. They have a list."

"The list will do them no good," Roan said. "He is safe where he is. Forgive me, Wil, but Ferus and I took an oath. No one is to know. Not even the Eleven." His gaze was steadfast, but Obi-Wan suddenly saw the color drain from his face, and he closed his eyes.

"He needs rest," Amie said.

Wil started reluctantly for the door. Obi-Wan

went with him, but paused at the door. "I just need another moment," he said in a low tone to Amie and Wil.

"Only a moment," Amie said.

"I know him," Wil said. "He will tell you nothing. Can you blame him? Somehow the Imperials found their case files. We could have a spy in the organization. We must investigate this."

Quietly, Wil and Amie left the room.

"I think I know who you are," Roan said, without opening his eyes. "He had no secrets from me. You are the Jedi Master Obi-Wan Kenobi, member of the Jedi High Council — former member, that is. He described you perfectly."

"How was that?"

"Tall and stubborn. And stiff."

"Stiff?"

"Stiff." Roan twisted in the bed and opened his eyes, his gaze suddenly penetrating. "The Jedi were wiped out, and yet you live. Why is that?"

"I was able to . . . avoid what happened."

Roan didn't drop his gaze. "How fortunate."

"What are you saying?"

"I've heard that some Jedi turned . . . they went to the dark side. How do I know you did not?"

"You don't," Obi-Wan said. "But the Ferus I knew had good instincts. Once, I did not listen to him, and

89

I am sorrier about that than you'll ever know. He knew, better than I did, how to listen to instincts. If you know him well, you know that, too."

He saw that Roan was hesitating. Despite Roan's words, Obi-Wan saw that the young man was aware that he would not be able to leave his bed for some time.

"I will not tell the Eleven. I'll tell no one. You must trust me," Obi-Wan said. "Ferus trusted me once. I am the one to do this. The struggle for this planet could be mirrored on thousands of other planets. We need to make a decisive move now, to show that the Empire cannot destroy the people's will."

"Ferus and I had a pact —"

"And do you think he is keeping it? He thinks you're still in prison. Do you think he's going to stay away?"

Roan closed his eyes again. "No," he said softly. "He won't stay away."

"I can't give you facts. You must make this decision based on nothing but your feelings."

"Now you sound like Ferus." Roan gave a deep sigh, and looked up at the ceiling. Obi-Wan could see the struggle on his face. "He is in the mountain region of Arno," he said. "I'll give you the coordinates. Find him. He won't admit it, but I'm sure he could use the help."

* * *

He waited for nightfall. During the daytime, the streets were too dangerous. Rilla gave him new ID docs and arranged for a starfighter to transport him — something that required her to call in all of her favors. He would be a businessman from Raed-7. The Eleven didn't know where he was going, but they would help him get there. They all agreed that until they knew if they'd been infiltrated, it was better to keep information safe.

"We still do much business with Raed-7," she explained. "They are building a pipeline network outside the city. They will question you, but your papers are in order. If they thought you had no reason to be here, they might detain you at the spaceport."

"This is the best way to leave Ussa," Wil agreed. "I'm sure, after today, outlanders will want to leave the city. There will be others there for cover."

Obi-Wan slipped the papers inside his traveling cloak.

"Safe journey," Rilla said.

"Tell Ferus not to return," Wil said. "If he is safe, then let him be safe. Tell him we will smuggle Roan out to him. He need not come back. He must know that Roan is safe."

"I will find him," Obi-Wan promised.

He walked to the spaceport. The streets were dark; the moon was covered with clouds. There were lights inside the buildings, but they were faint, as though the Bellassans inside were afraid to show too much evidence of their presence. Occasionally he would hear a patrol and melt back into a doorway or alley.

When he reached the spaceport, Obi-Wan was surprised to see that it was bustling. Beings pressed toward the checkpoint, many with bundles and baggage.

An Imperial officer with a malicious expression walked to the front. "All Bellassans must return to their homes. No Bellassans will be allowed to leave the planet. Ussa is in lockdown. Outlanders may approach the checkpoint."

"But my wife is in the Anturus system!"

"I have exit papers from the Imperial government on Coruscant!"

The cries erupted from the crowd.

The officer and his soldiers drew their blaster rifles and aimed them straight at the crowd. "Return to your homes!"

Obi-Wan saw a woman next to him tremble. A man put his hand on his young son's shoulder. Slowly, the residents began to move back, shouldering their baggage and herding their children.

He could not imagine why they thought they could get out. But they were desperate and willing to try anything.

Obi-Wan saw a squad of men dressed in dark

traveling clothes peel off from the few remaining beings at the checkpoint. He knew immediately they were Imperial spies, dressed to blend in. The Bellassans surging back toward the exit did not notice as the men slipped into their midst. They would follow them home. They would get their names. The Bellassans who tried to leave would go on a list, a list that would track them now as possible threats to the Empire.

"You there!" The officer pointed at him.

Obi-Wan stepped forward, holding out his ID docs. The officer jerked his head, pointing to the checkpoint. Obi-Wan handed over his ID docs.

He breathed evenly as the officer scrutinized them. He had to trust Rilla and Wil. It had been some time since he'd trusted anyone but himself.

"You've got the DP-x Explorer," the officer said. "Nice transport for a businessman."

"Got it in the Raed-7 spaceport market sale after the end of the Clone Wars," Obi-Wan replied, putting on a hearty voice. "What a sweet deal. Lots of beauties for sale back then. The pilots are dead — bad for them, good for me!"

"Right," the officer said expressionlessly. "You can proceed."

Obi-Wan walked off, tucking his ID docs back into his belt. He had only taken a few steps before he heard his name called.

"Ronar Hanare!"

He stopped and turned. It might have been a trick; he wasn't sure. Sometimes beings could get through a checkpoint with false ID docs, then forget their fake name in the relief of having made it through. The officer would call out the name to see how quickly they would react . . . or not.

"You have to file a flight plan before you leave," the officer said. His gaze was wary. Did he suspect something?

"Check," Obi-Wan said.

He let out a slow breath as he walked to his cruiser, a pleasure craft that had been converted to deep space capability. He surveyed his surroundings without seeming to look, a Jedi technique. Nothing seemed amiss. He felt no surge of the Force, warning him. Another solitary man, large and prosperous looking, was conferring with his pilot. No doubt he was another businessman, anxious to escape the turbulent planet. A shorter figure in a dark flight suit, his back to Obi-Wan, was running through an engine check on a gray cruiser. Obi-Wan recognized it as a Firespray-class ship, a rare model that appeared to have been customized.

Obi-Wan climbed into his transport. He quickly keyed in a flight plan to Raed-7 and sent it to the control system. When approval for takeoff flashed back, he wasted no time, but shot up into the planet's atmosphere.

He followed the flight plan up into space. He would make one orbit of the planet and then return to the atmosphere to get to the coordinates of Arno.

He looked down at the tracking screen. A ship had taken off behind him. It was heading his way, but staying back, lurking. Odd. It had a cloaked identity. He turned, trying to make visual contact through the windscreen of the cockpit.

It was the Firespray attack ship. Someone was following him — someone, he suddenly realized, with a connection to his past.

CHAPTER TWELVE

According to his flight plan, Obi-Wan was scheduled to jump to hyperspace. He decided to deviate slightly from that plan, and see what happened.

He stayed in realspace, plotting a lazy orbit around Bellassa. When the time came for his jump to hyperspace, he maintained cruising speed.

The Firespray ship increased speed. Obi-Wan followed suit.

The pilot must have customized the engine as well as the body of the craft.

Obi-Wan increased his speed to maximum. He was screaming across the sky now, and the ship just kept on coming. Soon, it would be within firing range. But surely he wouldn't be fired on . . .

An explosion rocked the ship. The controls were wrenched from his hands, and he nearly fell out of his chair. The Firespray had obviously customized weapons systems, too. Deadly ones. A proton torpedo had just detonated close to the ship.

Obi-Wan put his ship through evasive maneuvers as laser cannons sent streaks of deadly fire toward the ship. It had been so long since he'd done this, yet he had not forgotten anything — the feel of the controls, the knowledge of how far he could push the ship, the feeling in his stomach if a dive was too steep.

The Firespray continued to blast him. These weren't warning shots. Whoever the pilot was, he wanted to bring Obi-Wan down.

Obi-Wan pushed the ship through more corkscrew turns and dives, but he knew it was only a matter of time before the Firespray scored a hit.

If Anakin were here, he'd be piloting. This was the kind of challenge he enjoyed.

The thought had risen unbidden. He could not seem to stop such thoughts. He was still in the habit of thinking of his apprentice, his friend. Anakin. Not who he became.

He didn't want to remember. It brought too much pain.

With a quick glance at the nav computer, he saw that he was near the remote mountain range of Arno. He didn't want to lead the pursuer there, but if he was successful they wouldn't know he had landed. Now he pushed the engines that extra bit he knew they could handle, until he was momentarily out of range of his pursuer. Then, he dived toward the surface. If his pursuer had him on his tracking computer, he would merely think Obi-Wan was trying to lose him in the mountains, where the sensors would have trouble getting a fix on him.

He had only a few seconds before the Firespray would track him down visually. Obi-Wan hugged the mountainside, zooming up and over and down into the valley, skimming so close that he could almost count the snow crystals on the peaks. The steep inclines and deep valleys created wind currents that buffeted the ship.

Ice had sought out the deep crevices in the rocks and glinted blue below him. Giant bridges made of ice appeared, and he zoomed through them. He held onto his speed, but it was making the craft hard to handle. He kept his eyes on the surface of the snow below.

At last he spotted what he was looking for — what was most likely a meadow in the summer was now a vast snowfield. How deep, he wasn't sure — he was getting a variety of readings, meaning that drifts had formed. In some places the snow was fifty meters deep. He looked carefully at the surface. He could see no skin of ice, which meant he would not leave evidence of his landing. Yet the snow had to be packed hard enough for the ship to settle without sinking too far. He hoped.

Holding his breath, Obi-Wan aimed the ship straight down at top speed and then cut the power. The ship sailed with what seemed like great gentleness toward the bed of snow.

Then it hit. Obi-Wan's head jerked back with the impact. Sound seemed to be sucked into the snow itself. He heard the snow above fall with a whoosh down on the top of the cockpit. The whiteness surrounded him.

The ship settled down, the snow cascading, falling all around him. It was like being buried alive. The ship settled a few more meters, then stopped.

It was dark, but there was a curious quality to the light, slightly luminous despite the gloom. He saw his breath cloud the air. He waited. He would have to use his senses, not his instruments.

He called on the Force. His awareness moved up through the molecules of snow, through the spaces between the molecules, up into the thin air above. He could hear it or sense it — he wasn't sure, but he knew the Firespray was there, searching for him, flying back and forth over the mountains, dipping into the snow meadows and up again, buzzing like a frustrated insect.

After a time he felt the vacuum of its leaving. The Force smoothed out. He was alone.

Obi-Wan gazed outside the cockpit. He would not be able to take off from here. Even this ship, powerful as it was, would not be able to blast out against the snow. He would have to crawl out. He activated the canopy control. It struggled against the snow but did not rise. He took a deep breath and let it out. He would not allow himself to consider the possibility that he was trapped.

He put on his thermal cape and strapped on his survival pack. Then he took out his lightsaber and cut a hole in the canopy. Snow tumbled in, but he was able to crawl out. His landing had created a small bubble here, enough to breathe. He shoved a hand in the snow and tried to grab it. It would not hold him.

He tried to remember what was above. He reached for the grapnel line on his utility belt. It had a recoiling action, so he could shoot a filament above, but the claw end had to bite into something. He cleared a space above with his lightsaber, then shot the cable up at an angle, trying to pinpoint where he remembered seeing a small cluster of rocks.

The cable failed and recoiled back into the grapnel gun. He tried again. The recoiling action pulled the line back.

Again and again Obi-Wan shot the cable up into the air. The snow was starting to melt due to his body warmth and the fading warmth of the ship. Chunks of it collapsed on top of him. If he kept this up, he would start an avalanche above himself — small, but enough to bury him for good.

He shot it up again. This time, it held. He tested it. It had to work. He activated the mechanism, and the cable retracted, pulling him up through the snow. It got in his hair and his eyes and his mouth, but he did not stop moving.

He broke through to the surface and said hello to a gray sky. Obi-Wan lay flat on the snow. He pressed the mechanism and the filament recoiled. He tucked the grapnel line back into his belt. Then he rose slowly, gazing in awe at the vast mountains below and above him.

He dusted the snow off his tunic and started to walk.

Night was falling on the second day as he scaled the last cliff toward the coordinates Roan had given him. He had taken the most direct route, which meant much of the time he was making his way vertically, up cliff-sides and scaling huge boulders. He was exhausted and cold. His thermal cape was stiff with ice. Ice crystals had formed on his growing beard and eyelashes. But he was determined to finish his journey tonight.

At last he saw it — a small white stone cabin blending in with the snow. Relieved, he walked toward it.

A voice came from behind him. It was female, crisp.

"You've got a blaster rifle pointed at your back. Don't move."

"I'm a friend."

"I don't have friends."

"Roan sent me."

"Never heard of him."

He heard the unmistakable sound of a rifle being lifted to a shoulder. His hand went to his lightsaber.

The door to the cabin opened.

"Dona, don't shoot," Ferus said after a long pause. "I'm afraid my friend will take it very personally if you do."

CHAPTER THIRTEEN

Obi-Wan walked forward. The sight of Ferus struck him as slightly unreal.

"I thought you were dead," Ferus said.

"Perhaps I was," Obi-Wan responded.

To Obi-Wan's surprise, Ferus moved forward and embraced him. Ferus, who had always been so proper. It had been so long since Obi-Wan had felt an emotion like this that he feared he would be overwhelmed. He swallowed and hugged Ferus back. The rush of feeling felt like spring water down a parched throat. Ferus was alive, and that meant that the past had not died. Not completely.

Ferus stepped back and grinned. "And I thought I was immune to surprises." He turned to Dona. "So, what do you say? Do you think we should invite him in? You're the boss."

The woman didn't smile, but Obi-Wan could see that she enjoyed Ferus's teasing. "Looks like he could use a thawing out," she said. "Just don't get puddles on my floor."

"I'll tell you one thing," Ferus said in an undertone to Obi-Wan. "I know there'll be soup."

Ferus drew him into the warmth of the house. Now that they were in the light, Obi-Wan could see the changes in him. He was leaner, more muscled. His face had matured; its angles were sharper. He was still only in his early twenties, but the wide gold streak in his dark hair had turned to silver. He gave the impression of a man who had been through things he would not want to talk about.

But there was a looseness to him, too, which was new. Even his walk was different. Once, Ferus had moved with the rigid assurance that came with a disciplined mind. Now he hooked a chair with his foot and dragged it in front of the fire and waved Obi-Wan toward it. The old Ferus would never have done something so casual, and so . . . graceful. And Obi-Wan had never heard Ferus joke before. He had changed in ways Obi-Wan had yet to discover.

"You're staring," Ferus said.

"I'm sorry, it's that you seem so different."

"You, too. You've gone completely gray. You look older. In fact, you don't look all that well."

"Thanks."

As soon as Obi-Wan's wet things were whisked

away by Dona, and he was sitting in front of the warm fire, Ferus allowed his anxiety to show.

"You said that Roan sent you," Ferus said.

"He is fine," Obi-Wan said. "He was smuggled out of the med clinic and taken to the Eleven. He was . . . given some neurotoxins while in prison."

Ferus nodded grimly.

"But we were able to discover what they were, and he's awake now. Getting stronger by the minute. He asked me to tell you not to return to Ussa. There were mass arrests the day I left. It isn't safe there."

Ferus sighed and sank into a chair opposite Obi-Wan. "I hate the Empire. And I hate this exile."

"You can't stay here," Obi-Wan said. "The Imperials are checking your list of clients. Roan thinks you are safe, but I'm not sure. . . ."

"Dona isn't on the list on our computer files."

"I was followed from Ussa. I don't know why or by whom. I don't know if it has anything to do with you, but we can't take any chances."

Ferus nodded, frowning. "Where is your transport?"

"Buried under a snowbank."

"Dona has tools, we can get it out. You're right — I should leave. Events have changed things. I'll have to get back in contact with the Eleven. We'll have to wait a bit longer for our chance, but we should be making plans."

Obi-Wan held out a hand for the bowl Dona brought to him. His cold fingers curled around the heat. He had forgotten this, too — how warmth and safety felt after an impossible journey. "Just what do you expect to accomplish?"

"I expect to overthrow the Empire, one planet at a time," Ferus answered. "Nothing less than that."

As Ferus eased himself back into the chair, Obi-Wan could see that he was still in pain.

"It's nothing," Ferus said, seeing Obi-Wan glance at his leg. "I was wounded in the escape. Caught a bit of blasterfire. Dona's been treating it, and it's almost healed."

"I'm sensing something that surprises me," Obi-Wan said slowly. "I would not expect that life outside the Jedi Order would suit you."

"I would have said the same," Ferus said with a laugh. "But I adjusted. Siri used to always tell me that I must accept change. Welcome it, she said — change is what keeps the galaxy spinning. It's what makes it beautiful." Ferus looked into the fire. "I heard about her death, before all the others. I'm sorry, Obi-Wan."

"There were so many deaths," Obi-Wan said. Ferus didn't know, but Obi-Wan missed Siri constantly and intensely, even still.

"I'm sorry, I have to ask, Obi-Wan — Anakin. He didn't survive either?"

Obi-Wan couldn't tell him. He would tell a version of the truth. "He didn't survive." The Anakin they both knew was dead. "He was hunted down by the Empire."

Ferus nodded, pain in his gaze, even though he and Anakin had been rivals more than friends. "I had thought that leaving the Jedi would be the most terrible occurrence of my life," he said. "It turns out to have saved my life. I was not among those caught at the Temple, or on another planet. I wasn't hunted down. But hearing about all that . . . it was hard to bear. Betrayal. And seeing the galaxy in the grip of the Emperor — that is something that eats at me. What could we have done, what could we have seen?"

"We do not look back. We take each moment."

Ferus stretched out his legs. "Ah yes, so the Jedi say. So where have you been for the past year or so?"

"Here and there," Obi-Wan said. He trusted Ferus, but he would not tell him about Luke and Leia. The more a secret was told, the less a secret it became.

"Ah, I won't ask," Ferus said. "I'm just glad to see you. Do you know if any other Jedi have survived?"

Obi-Wan hesitated. The fact that Yoda was still alive was another secret. "I know of only one for sure, who I cannot mention," he said. "There might be some who have gone underground. There's no way to tell. There was a beacon calling Jedi back to the Temple, to be slaughtered. We managed to replace it with a signal saying to stay away — but at that point, it may have been too late. There may not be any others left."

Ferus leaned forward, forearms on his knees, hands clasped. "I find that hard to believe. There's got to be a way to find them. The Jedi were too powerful to be completely wiped out. There must be others who survived, just as you did. I think of that question. It haunts me."

Obi-Wan shook his head. "I'm sorry, Ferus. It is impossible to believe, but you must believe it. The Jedi are gone."

The firelight glinted in Ferus's dark gaze, licking it with orange. "I will never believe it," he said. "And now that you're here, we can do something about it."

Obi-Wan was already shaking his head. "I have my own task to fulfill. I will help you now, but then I must leave and never return."

"You can't mean that."

"I do."

"But there is so much to fight for."

"My days of fighting are over, for now."

"What can be more important?"

Obi-Wan didn't answer.

"I don't like having to question a Jedi Master,"

Ferus said. "Old habits die hard. But are you kidding me? You'd rather hide than fight?"

The words and the manner shocked Obi-Wan. He kept silent in disapproval.

"Now don't get all Jedi-proper on me," Ferus said. "I can see it on your face. I'm not your apprentice, Obi-Wan. You deserve my respect, of course. But I've learned to speak frankly. This is a new reality, a new galaxy."

"We fought and died in the new galaxy," Obi-Wan said, feeling a prick of irritation.

"I know that," Ferus said. "What I meant is that the galaxy has changed. To choose exile over engagement dooms us all to domination and despair."

"Ferus, I'm not one of the Eleven," Obi-Wan said. "I'm an old friend. I didn't come here to be recruited."

"So what is your answer to the Empire?"

Obi-Wan looked into the fire. He could feel the word on his lips, but he didn't want to say it. He knew it would infuriate Ferus. "Wait."

"Wait?"

Ferus looked as though he wanted to leap out of the chair and throttle Obi-Wan. Obi-Wan held his gaze steadily. The galaxy may have been different, but he still knew how to subdue a turbulent apprentice.

Ferus suddenly smiled and leaned back against the cushion Dona had placed behind him. "I remember when that look used to scare me. It almost scares me now. *Almost*, Obi-Wan."

Ferus spoke so amiably that Obi-Wan felt his irritation drain away. Of course Ferus wouldn't understand his decision.

Obi-Wan sipped his soup. "There is something else I must tell you," he said. "There is an Imperial security officer, an Inquisitor named Malorum —"

"Yes, I've met him," Ferus said. "He was there for the interrogations, though he didn't speak."

"He has a Force connection."

Ferus nodded slowly. "I suspected that . . . I wasn't sure. It's been so long since I've used the Force. It's still part of me, but I don't access it."

"Do you know anything about him?"

"I know he's distinguished himself at the highest level," Ferus said. "He's said to be Lord Vader's special pet. He can choose his own assignments."

"He is very interested in capturing you, that much I know," Obi-Wan said.

"Well, he'll just have to be disappointed," Ferus said. "I don't intend to revisit an Imperial jail cell again." He picked up his spoon. "Now, I suggest we do as the Jedi do . . ."

Obi-Wan smiled. "When food arrives, eat."

* * *

Obi-Wan thought he would have trouble sleeping, but the rest his body craved overtook him. Wrapped in Dona's hand-loomed blankets, he fell asleep by the warmth of the fire.

In the morning, Obi-Wan had a glimpse through the window of an impossibly wide blue sky, white-capped mountains in the distance.

"Dona doesn't like me to open the armorweave curtains, but over here we can't be seen on the mountainside," Ferus said, once Obi-Wan was up. "Did you sleep well?"

"Yes, thank you," Obi-Wan said. He thought it strange to be having such an ordinary conversation, guest to host, under these circumstances. It felt so normal, when the situation was anything but normal. Obi-Wan still wasn't used to the new position he found himself in. Ferus was no longer a Padawan. Every rule that had bound them together was gone.

Dona hurried into the kitchen, clutching her morning robe to her throat. "There is news," she said. "I was able to access the HoloNet."

Ferus snorted. "We can't believe anything we hear on that. It's controlled by the Empire."

"I'm afraid this is all too true," Dona said. "The mass arrests in Ussa . . . the Empire has issued an ultimatum. If the city does not give up Ferus Olin within twenty-four hours, everyone held in the mass arrest will be executed. The order came down six hours ago."

The color faded from Ferus's face. His body went rigid.

"So that was why they did it," Obi-Wan said. "They arrested so many in order to catch only one."

"I have to go back," Ferus said. "I have to give myself up."

CHAPTER FOURTEEN

He didn't have a choice. If he didn't do it, innocent people would die. Even as he got up from the table, Ferus frantically began to calculate how long it would take him to get to Ussa. Dona didn't have a cruiser capable of going that far, but she had a friend in the village . . .

"Wait," Obi-Wan said, putting a hand on his arm.

All of Ferus's fury at the Empire funneled down into the man standing before him, blocking his way.

"Is that all you can do — wait? I have to leave now!" Ferus couldn't believe that Obi-Wan was the same Jedi he once knew. He remembered Obi-Wan as cautious, but this was ridiculous.

"I just mean you should consider how you return," Obi-Wan began. "There might be a way to —"

A soft alarm suddenly rang on the databoard in Dona's kitchen. "Penetration," she said. "Someone is in the airspace. Let me survey —"

An explosion sent debris raining down on them while a wall of air sent them flying. Ferus sailed backward in what seemed like slow motion, riding a cushion of air. He landed hard on the kitchen floor, his head banging on the counter behind him. He saw the table flying toward him, and he knew with a cold certainty he was able to grasp in less than a second that it would fall on his injured leg. He reached out for the Force, but it was a blind, instinctive gesture without any power behind it. He could feel the Force, but not access it.

To his surprise, the table flew across the room. He saw Obi-Wan had Force-pushed it even as he himself hit the floor. It fell inside the small crater where once there had been a hand-hooked rug.

Above his head he could see blue sky. The assault had punched a hole in the reinforced roof.

Obi-Wan was already moving, glancing through the window as Dona waved a frantic hand over the sensor for the armorweave curtains.

"It's the Firespray that tailed me from Ussa."

Ferus gently grabbed Dona's hand. "It's too late," he said. "I don't think the curtains are going to stop this."

She looked up at the space where most of the roof had been. "Of course."

"Do you have a transport?" Obi-Wan asked her.

"Nothing that can outrun that," Dona said.

"And we have no cover if we run," Obi-Wan said.

"We don't have to run," Dona said. "The house can withstand attack for a time, but we'd better not stay. This way."

It was then that the door blew open in a blast that sent them all diving for cover.

Behind an overturned chair, Ferus peered toward the door. A creature blocked out the light from outside. It was a cyborg, its body covered in armor. But there was a laser cannon where the head should have been. It aimed directly at him. He saw the red targeting light pulse.

So there were two of them. One in the air, one on the ground. This was definitely not good news.

Obi-Wan was a blur of movement, his lightsaber a slashing glow. He barreled forward, aiming for the being's head. The being had to step away, ruining his aim. The laser cannon boomed, but it missed Ferus and thudded into the kitchen sink. Water shot into the air, and flames erupted.

"Go!" Obi-Wan shouted.

Ferus helped Dona to rise. Together they rushed from the kitchen. Even as he moved to bring Dona to safety, Ferus's mind worked furiously. He couldn't leave Obi-Wan.

Ferus raced to a hidden compartment in the hallway wall. He knew where all the weaponry was concealed in the house. He slung a blaster rifle over his arm and loaded his pockets with C16 grenades. He tossed Dona a few, and she tucked them in her belt. He knew she always had a blaster strapped to her ribs. He slid out an electrojabber and held it by his side as he hurried her along down the hall, blasterfire ripping through the roof over their heads and blasting through the floorboards.

Dona reached the trapdoor hidden in the floor and pressed the release. Ferus helped her inside the opening. "Go," he said. "Get to the village. They don't want you. Only me."

"I can't leave you."

He took both of her hands in his as the house shuddered with the impact of another laser cannon blast. "You have done enough. More than enough. I'll never forget it. Plus, this house is about to be destroyed. Now get out of here."

She let go of his hands and slid down the ramp.

Ferus raced back to the kitchen. In a glance, he saw that Obi-Wan had succeeded in keeping the intruder trapped in the doorway. The intruder, meanwhile, had succeeded in destroying the kitchen. Fire blazed along one wall, and the other was partially demolished. Obi-Wan was busy avoiding the strafing fire from the attacking ship above and the pounding of the laser cannon on the creature's head.

Ferus used the electrojabber like a javelin, and threw it. It smashed into the creature's chest and stayed there. Although the cyborg was armored, the force of the blow sent it staggering backward and paralyzed it momentarily. It crashed to its knees.

"This way!" Ferus shouted to Obi-Wan.

He had left the trapdoor open. Obi-Wan sailed in and slid down the ramp. Ferus followed, hitting the control as he went. The trapdoor slid smoothly shut after them.

Sound became muffled as they slid down to the floor and got to their feet.

"There's an entrance to the old mining tunnels we can access down here."

"Where's Dona?" Obi-Wan asked.

"I sent her ahead to the village. We'd better not go that way. If they do manage to find the tunnels, we should lead them away from her."

Obi-Wan nodded. "Let's get moving."

Ferus put his hand on what appeared to be sheer rock. The sensor was exactly where Dona had showed him. The hidden door opened smoothly, and they stepped inside.

"These used to be mutonium mines, before the mineral ran out. There's a maze of tunnels all through the mountains. Dona explored them when she first arrived here — she knows them like the back of her hand. She gave me a lesson on direction a couple of days after I arrived, in case I had to escape alone. I have a general idea of how to get to the other side of the mountain. Maybe they won't figure out how to get down here."

"Somehow I doubt that," Obi-Wan said. "Lead on."

Ferus started down the tunnel. The miners had blasted through rock to form the tunnels, and they were reinforced with large durasteel beams that served as supports. The glow lamps no longer worked, but Ferus's eyes adjusted quickly, and they were able to move faster.

"Do you think they followed you here?"

"No," Obi-Wan said. "No one tailed me from the landing spot. They found you another way. The cyborg with the laser cannon for a head —"

"Handsome creature. Charming way to introduce oneself. Why knock when you can blast a door down?"

"— any ideas on who sent him?"

"I heard a rumor in prison, that Malorum had a team of bounty hunters working for him. One was called D'harhan, a cyborg that was more like a walking assault weapon. Must be him. I never heard about a Firespray."

But Obi-Wan had an idea about the second one . . . .

"I wish I knew what was happening up there," Obi-Wan said, with a glance up at the tunnel ceiling.

"Once you closed the door to the mines behind you, it activated a warning. The next one who tries to open it will detonate a small explosive charge," Ferus explained as he hurried down the tunnel. "We should be able to hear it down here. Then we'll know they found the tunnel."

Ferus's heart was pounding, but it wasn't the aftermath of the assault. All he could think of was the citizens of Ussa slated for execution. "Every minute I spend down here is a minute I'm not traveling to Ussa. The executions are scheduled to start in less than a day."

"You must focus on the present moment," Obi-Wan said. "Not on what *might* happen."

"Obi-Wan, I'm warning you," Ferus said. "If you keep sounding like a Jedi Code doc, we are really not going to get along."

"So, what are we looking for?" Obi-Wan asked.

"Water. I know there's an exit by an underground lake."

They kept on going, pressing on. Suddenly, they heard a muffled thump.

"I guess they found the door," Ferus muttered.

They quickened their pace, almost running now.

Ferus doubted the explosion had stopped them. Although it would be a nice bonus if it had blown that laser cannon into a few choice pieces of scrap.

"Even if they survived that blast, there's no way they can find us," Ferus finally said. "The tunnels are a maze, and they'll get lost. *I'm* lost. There's no way they —"

They heard the whistle of the rocket behind them. They dived to the floor as it zoomed overhead and thudded into the rock. The ceiling tilted, and rocks rained down, but the tunnel did not collapse.

"You were saying?" Obi-Wan asked.

"Who *are* those guys?" Ferus asked, coughing out the grit from his lungs, and they started to run.

CHAPTER FIFTEEN

The smaller one wore armor, a helmet, and wrist and knee rockets. Obi-Wan could deflect the blaster fire with his lightsaber, but that meant he had to keep turning, and the only thing that could protect them from the laser cannon was running. Luckily, their pursuers had to be somewhat careful. Too much cannonfire could bring down the tunnel on all of them.

He hadn't used his lightsaber in so many long months. Yet it felt perfectly balanced in his hand, and his movements were quick and graceful. He was able to run and twist to deflect fire, able to leap and whirl, his lightsaber in a controlled arc of movement, and not have to think about how to accomplish it. He was fighting like a Jedi again.

Ferus ran fast, but Obi-Wan could detect a slight hitch in his stride, proof that his leg was not healed enough to keep up a constant pace. They needed to lose their pursuers, not outrun them.

"Do you smell it?" Ferus said over the sound of blasterfire. "Water."

"We can't go straight toward it," Obi-Wan said, swinging his lightsaber. "We need to get a head start."

"One or two of these side tunnels must come out there, too," Ferus said. "It's just a question of choosing the right one."

Obi-Wan accessed the Force. The smell of water, of damp, was faint. He was surprised Ferus had picked it up, but he could also sense the stirring of the Force in him. Even as he ran and kept his lightsaber whirling, he concentrated on the smell until it filled a part of his consciousness so completely that he could track it. "Third tunnel on the left up ahead," he said. "After the curve. Let's try a diversion."

Ferus tossed a grenade backward with a spinning accuracy that impressed Obi-Wan. He had timed it to fall short, but the two attackers didn't know that. The grenade hit, blowing a large hole in the hard-packed floor and sending the younger bounty hunter flying backward. The cyborg was stronger and absorbed the blow, but lurched forward and fell into the hole.

Smoke and dirt particles filled the tunnel. Ferus

and Obi-Wan used it as cover to make a dash for the side tunnel. They moved off silently down the narrower passage. They could just make out the sound of their pursuers racing down the main tunnel. They had lost them — for now.

The dark, narrow tunnel had deteriorated over the years. They waded through puddles of water and had to step over fallen beams. The blackness was complete. It was as though they'd been buried in the heart of the mountain. But at least they weren't dodging laser fire.

The smell of damp grew stronger. At last Obi-Wan saw a glimmer ahead. The lake.

They emerged into a huge, arching cavern of dark red stone. Towering needles of rock surrounded them like a forest. A lake with water as black as oil lapped at the smooth stone of the floor. Across the lake they could see the continuation of the tunnel, its entrance partially blocked with fallen supports.

"The good news is that we found it," Ferus said. "The bad news is that we have to swim across it."

Obi-Wan handed Ferus an aquata rebreather. "We'll have to share this. We'll have to stay underwater to avoid detection. By the looks of that water, we won't be able to see a thing. Do you think you can access the Force?"

Ferus shook his head. "I've been trying, but . . ."

Obi-Wan reached into his belt and withdrew the

grapnel line. He let out a short length of the strong filament and hooked the claw into Ferus's belt. "Hang onto this, then."

The water was shockingly cold. Obi-Wan slipped under the surface. He felt his skin shrink from the terrible cold. He hoped Ferus could make it. Water this cold could cause cramping or paralysis. Without the Force to help him, Ferus might have trouble swimming.

He began to stroke across the lake, feeling the occasional tug of the cable line that meant Ferus was swimming behind him. Occasionally Ferus would tug the line and pass the rebreather up to Obi-Wan. He dived as deep as he dared, not wanting even a ripple to announce their presence underneath the water.

Midway across the lake he felt the cable line grow taut. He turned, barely able to make out the shadow that was Ferus behind him.

Ferus was in trouble. The combination of the cold and his injury was making it difficult for him to swim. He was struggling, and Obi-Wan could see the effort it cost him.

He reached under Ferus's arms and began to stroke with one hand, pulling Ferus along through the water. The effort was exhausting. He reached out to the Force, gathering it from the water and the rocks and the air above. He wanted to ride it like a wave to the safety of the opposite shore. He didn't want to take the aquata rebreather from Ferus; he could feel Ferus struggling for breath. But he couldn't hold out much longer without it.

Then Obi-Wan felt a surprising thing. The Force was meeting the Force, a weak attempt, to be sure, but Ferus was accessing it, nurturing it, trying to use it to join with Obi-Wan. Perhaps it helped him to have their bodies joined together, for Obi-Wan felt the Force grow. And then the Force was pulsing between them and around them, binding them together, the two of them, and making them one with the molecules of water in the lake so that they slipped through the water with ease.

Obi-Wan looked over at Ferus. He nodded at Obi-Wan, pleased at what had happened, even amid the freezing water and the danger. He had found the Force again. He handed Obi-Wan the rebreather and they began to share it again.

Soon Obi-Wan could feel, rather than see, that they were close to the other side. Now they would have to take the chance and expose themselves. There was enough light for their pursuers to see them if they were looking in this direction. They would have to do this silently.

Obi-Wan rose from the lake, just his head above the surface. He saw the two bounty hunters immediately. Their backs were to the lake, and they were circling, trying to discover where Obi-Wan and Ferus had gone.

Obi-Wan's memory pricked. He knew the smaller one. Something about the way he carried himself . . . His helmet obscured his face, but he was familiar to Obi-Wan. He studied his armor. It was green Mandalorian battle armor, and those were Kelvarek rocket systems on his wrist guards.

He looked like a smaller version of Jango Fett. But Jango Fett was dead.

But he had a son . . . a clone. Boba.

Boba must not see him. He would recognize him. He had met Boba when he was just a boy, on Kamino, but Obi-Wan could still feel the flat stare of the boy, how it seemed to take all of him in. And after the battle on Geonosis, when he had seen his father cut down by Mace Windu, no doubt the Jedi were no friends of this boy. How old could he be now? Thirteen, fourteen? Just a boy, but more than a boy. Another orphan of the Clone Wars, another boy taking on adulthood too soon.

He remembered Jango Fett's ship — it had been a Firespray. Retrofitted with increased weaponry, speed, targeting systems. It had been repainted.

All these thoughts raced through Obi-Wan's mind even as he nudged Ferus, who came up silently. They moved through the water, walking now, pushing gently against the water but not letting even the tiniest splash sound.

They were almost to the entrance of the tunnel when they were spotted. The laser cannon boomed. Cannonfire sprayed the water, sending them diving below the surface again, trying to keep their bodies under the shallow water.

Obi-Wan heard the *boom* as cannonfire hit the tunnel supports. The water rolled back, a wave that swept them into deeper water. The time to make their move was now, before they were trapped underwater while Boba Fett made his way toward them. They had to run for it.

Ferus was right with him. They did not need to look at each other or signal each other. They were of one mind now, one purpose.

Ferus burst through the surface of the water at the same time as Obi-Wan, and charged through the knee-deep water. Behind them, Boba Fett activated his jetpack. He rose into the air toward them.

Using the Force, Obi-Wan created a wave behind them. He reached out to every molecule of water, calling on the Force to bind them into a giant, cresting black wave. He felt Ferus join the effort, and the power of the wave picked them up and hurled them forward toward the tunnel.

The tunnel was now almost completely collapsed,

two durasteel columns knocked down, forming a cross that blocked the opening. Dirt and rocks were now falling from the ceiling to create more obstacles.

Boba Fett set off a concussion missile, aiming for the tunnel entrance. The impact was tremendous. The other support started to fall, the ceiling partially caving in.

Obi-Wan and Ferus careened through, carried by the cresting wave. They swam through the remaining space of the collapsing tunnel as the entrance smashed to the ground behind them, sealing them inside.

Obi-Wan's face slammed into the muddy ground, and he tasted lake water, dirt, and metallic rock in his mouth. He felt dirt thud onto his back and hoped he wouldn't be buried alive.

The noise stopped. Slowly, he rolled over, the dirt and rocks cascading off him.

"Ferus?"

Ferus's eyes were closed. His face was streaked with dirt, his cheek against the rock. Obi-Wan put a hand on his arm. "Ferus!"

His eyes opened. "That was . . . quite a ride," he managed to get out.

"Come on. Even a blocked tunnel won't stop those two. I recognized the other one. Boba Fett, a bounty hunter. He's just a kid, maybe fourteen or fifteen."

"Some kid," Ferus said, wincing as he got to his feet.

"Which way?"

"I'm not sure . . . to the left, I think."

They stumbled on. They'd gone less than a hundred meters when they heard another *boom.*

"They're not trying to chase us," Ferus said. "They're going to collapse the tunnel."

They might well succeed. Obi-Wan saw the durasteel supports shake. Rocks tumbled down onto the path. The ground shook.

Behind them, the tunnel caved in. Over their heads, the supports groaned.

"Run!" Ferus shouted.

They ran, speeding down the tunnel as the beams cracked overhead and supports began to topple.

Ahead, they saw a flash of color. It was Dona, still dressed in her morning robe, violet as the snow at twilight. Her gray hair streamed down her back.

"Hurry!" she called. "This way!"

"What are you doing?" Ferus asked her, as they ran up. "I told you we could take care of this."

"And you're doing so well," she replied.

Another explosion rocked the tunnel. The durasteel support behind them crashed to the ground. Obi-Wan grabbed Dona and Force-leaped, Ferus right beside him. They landed in the next tunnel while the rocks and dirt rained behind them.

"This tunnel isn't going to last much longer," Dona said. "Come on."

With Dona to direct them, they were able to race along the tunnels faster than before. The ground shook with every explosion, but she quickly led them down a side tunnel to a lift tube with an open cage.

"Does it work?" Ferus asked.

"Sure hope so. Get in." Dona jumped in and flipped the lever. As the cage rose smoothly, she grinned. "Only kidding. I keep this one running, just in case."

The hum of the machinery was reassuring. Obi-Wan looked down, glad to leave the tunnels below. The lift rocketed to the surface, shaking with each new blast.

Dona led them out of the tube into a small structure built into the rock of the mountain. They walked out into bright sunshine. They were high above the village here.

"We'll hike down the mountain to the village. I've got a friend with a fast speeder. It will get you to Ussa."

"We have less than sixteen hours," Ferus said.

CHAPTER SIXTEEN

It took more time than the impatient Ferus could bear, but at last they were in the two-seat speeder, streaking toward Ussa. There was no sign of Boba Fett and his lethal companion. But Obi-Wan knew he would have to make things right here — and then return as stealthily as possible to Tatooine.

"I have to warn you, " Obi-Wan now said to Ferus, "you may give yourself up, but there's no guarantee that Malorum will free the prisoners. I'm afraid it might be just the opposite."

"What do you mean? They can't go back on a deal."

"They can do whatever they like," Obi-Wan said quietly. "Surely you know that by now. They are perfectly capable of executing every prisoner. Including you. They know they need to strike fear into the hearts of every person in Ussa. They want to destroy you, and they want to destroy the spirit of the citizens. Giving yourself up won't save them. I saw a file in the garrison. It dealt with . . . how to hide a great number of deaths. Dispose of bodies."

Ferus looked horrified. "They can't murder all of them."

"Ferus, the extent of their evil is greater than you know," Obi-Wan said. "The evil begins at the top and trickles down. Emperor Palpatine is a Sith Lord."

"A Sith?" Ferus looked at him, shocked. The knowledge clicked in behind his eyes. "The Sith we were tracking . . . my last mission on Korriban . . ."

"Yes, but keep this to yourself. It was Count Dooku who Granta Omega was meeting. That's why, when Omega died, he told me I would wish I knew what he knew. About the identity of the Sith Lord."

Ferus was silent for some time. "So he planned this for some time. And Darth Vader . . ."

"Is his apprentice." Obi-Wan felt a spasm of pain. He didn't know if he would reveal Vader's identity to Ferus. There was no need for him to know.

"The Sith control the galaxy," Ferus said. "It is far, far worse than I thought. I thought we were fighting . . . an ordinary evil. So this is why the Jedi were destroyed. You were the only ones with the power to defeat him."

"Yes. So you see, I believe them capable of anything. Malorum is not a Sith, but the dark side is part of him. They will find some excuse for the executions. Then they're planning to shut down all comm systems on Bellassa. Embargo any information from leaving for a month. Close down the spaceport, isolate the planet completely. Eliminate all evidence. Then, if the news gets out, they can deny it. Ussa will be an example to the rest of the galaxy. This is part of a much, much bigger plan."

Ferus was silent for a long time. They had passed through the mountains and were now speeding along a vast empty plain. Ferus appeared to be concentrating on his piloting, as though they were moving through space traffic instead of empty air.

"First I must see Roan. Then I'll contact them. I trust everything you told me, Obi-Wan, but I have to give myself up. What choice do I have?"

"There is always more than one choice. At the risk of irritating you again, I want to remind you of some Jedi wisdom," Obi-Wan said.

"I'm not a Jedi anymore."

"Really?" Obi-Wan said. "Then I must have imagined your command of the Force back in the tunnels."

"I'd hardly use the word command," Ferus said. "I was like a bantha calf."

"You can get it back," Obi-Wan said. "You've already begun. What you know has not been lost."

"Maybe I wanted it to be lost," Ferus said.

"Maybe having the Force be a part of me was too hard after I left the Jedi."

"Now you can use it. You need it. It will be there."

"So, give me your wisdom, then, Obi-Wan," Ferus said. He propped one foot on the cockpit as he gripped the controls.

"Do what you must, but in an unexpected way."

"Ah. The first lesson of lightsaber training."

"No, the first lesson of lightsaber training was — don't fall down."

Ferus laughed softly. "I remember. "

"Then you must remember this — everything you learn in lightsaber training —"

"— can be used in life training," Ferus completed.

There was a short silence. "But what," Ferus said, "would be an unexpected way to give myself up?"

"At last," Obi-Wan said, "you have asked the right question."

Ferus stood at Roan's bedside.

"Hey, partner."

"Hey, partner."

"Any excuse for a lie down, I'd say."

Roan smiled. "Well, I sure never got a day off, working with you."

"He's doing better every hour," Amie Antin said.

Roan looked hard at Ferus. "You're giving yourself up, aren't you?"

"Yes, but not in the way you'd expect." Ferus turned to Obi-Wan. "My old friend has a plan."

Wil, Rilla, and Amie looked over at him.

"We can't take the deal at face value," Obi-Wan said. "If we do, everyone will die. Instead, we will ensure that everyone will live."

"How?" Wil asked.

"By using what you already have, not what you think you need," Obi-Wan said.

"What do we have?" Wil asked. "We don't have many weapons, or ships . . ."

"All we have is each other," Rilla said.

"Exactly," Obi-Wan said. "And that is all you need."

CHAPTER SEVENTEEN

Obi-Wan took Ferus to the narrow, entwined streets of the Moonstone District. Wrapped in a cloak, Ferus passed through the streets without being recognized.

"What are we doing here?" Ferus asked, a hint of impatience in his voice. "I'm running out of time. . . ."

"You have seven more hours."

"So you want to go shopping?"

"We're going to meet up with someone," Obi-Wan said. "A friend of yours, who, by the way, asked me to pass along a message to you."

"What's that?"

"'You stink like a bantha.'"

Ferus took this in, then laughed. "Trever? The kid who was always hanging around the office?"

They turned a corner into the alley and saw the

boy, just struggling to push his gravsled out from its parking space behind a garbage container.

Trever looked up and saw Obi-Wan.

"No," Trever said. "No, no, and no."

Ferus threw back the hood of his cloak.

Trever paled, and took a step back. "You're alive." Relief flooded his face, and it told Obi-Wan everything he needed to know.

"We need to talk," Obi-Wan told Trever.

Trever took them to the place where he slept at night — Obi-Wan didn't think the word "home" described it. He led them down another alley to a gray door, which he opened with a code.

"The foreman lets me sleep here," he said. "I give him a deal on stuff." He pushed open the door to a closet. The room was surprisingly warm.

"It's next to the heaters," Trever explained. "Nice in the wintertime. Have a seat."

The room was furnished with a rolled-up sleep mat in a corner and one chair. The only other place to sit was the floor, so Ferus and Obi-Wan sat down. Trever sat down next to them.

"Can I get you something? Frosted cakes? Juice of the dewflower?" Trever grinned. "Just kidding. I don't have anything."

His joke seemed forced, and Obi-Wan thought he knew why.

"What did you steal from the Olin/Lands office?" he asked Trever.

Trever's face seemed to close down. "Nothing."

Ferus went still. Trever didn't look at him.

"Right before Ferus and Roan were arrested."

"I told you, nothing," Trever said. "Is this why you came? Because —"

"Trever, it's all right," Obi-Wan said. "I think you need to tell Ferus. Was it something small, something you thought they wouldn't miss?"

"I thought it was no big deal," Trever said in a rush. "I thought . . . I thought it was something they were going to throw away. An old power droid with a busted motivator. They used to use it for backup power, but they put it in the junk pile."

Ferus put his head in his hands.

"You were throwing it away! Everything else I left alone, so in case they came back, they'd find it just like it was. The Imperials took away their datapads and their files, so I thought, a broken droid . . . I could just sell it on the black market."

"The droid," Ferus said. "We planted our coded files into the motivator. There's a way to access a data card. . . . It makes the motivator look broken. It was our secret system."

"Who did you sell it to?"

"Just another kid. I was in the district, and he

asked if I had any equipment for sale. I didn't think . . ."

Obi-Wan glanced at Ferus. "I think that boy was Boba Fett. I think he found out that Trever was in and out of your office. I think he found the files, and brought them to Malorum, and they were able to break the code. That's how Malorum knew that you and Roan had founded the Eleven. That's how they found your list of clients. Not the list on your datapad, but the real list . . . the list that included Dona." He turned back to Trever. "And you knew it. You suspected that you'd sold the droid to the wrong person."

"I didn't know for sure," Trever mumbled. "But yeah, I guessed it. I mean, Ferus and Roan were arrested right after. You were always straight with me, Ferus. I wouldn't have done it to you on purpose, even for all the credits on Bellassa. I mean, I'd steal from you from time to time, but I wouldn't turn you in."

"Now you can make up for it," Obi-Wan said. "You can help Ferus."

"How?"

Obi-Wan outlined what he needed. Trever was already shaking his head before Obi-Wan had finished.

"This is the craziest idea I've ever heard," he said. "Anyway, why do you need me?"

"Because you know Mariana's routine," Obi-Wan said. "And you know where, and how, to steal what we need."

"Look," Trever said. "I'm sorry for what I did to you, Ferus. But I don't stick my neck out. That's how I survive."

Ferus leaned in closer. "We're asking you to do something that's hard," he said. "You think resistance is futile. That's what they want you to think. You think if you just take care of yourself, that is enough. That's what they want you to think. So you make your life safe, and you follow their rules. That's what they want you to do. And meanwhile, they steal your homeworld right from under your nose. And they tell you that your life is better. They tell you that they're giving you peace and freedom, and they expect you to buy what they're selling you. They're counting on you to be quiet, to listen to their HoloNet and believe their lies. Are you going to give them what they want?"

Obi-Wan looked at Ferus. This was the charismatic leader the others had spoken of, the man who spoke plainly but could inspire. He could see the change in Trever, he could see how the boy raised his head as purpose flooded him again.

"I'll do it," he said. His eyes gleamed at Ferus. "But don't think it's because you convinced me. It's because I like a good show."

On the surface, the city had not changed. The Ussans came home from work, ate their evening meal, watched over their children. But beneath these ordinary things another purpose hummed. After months and months of helplessness, the people of Ussa were asked to risk. And they responded.

Ferus sent a message to the garrison. He would surrender at daybreak, but on one condition — that all the prisoners be released first.

He would stand outside the gates of the garrison, on the Commons. When every one of the prisoners had walked out, he would walk in.

Just before dawn, Obi-Wan sat in a small airspeeder in an alleyway off the Commons. The people of Ussa were thick in the streets. The Commons area in front of the garrison had been cleared by the stormtroopers, who stood outside the garrison gates, force pikes pointed out toward the crowd.

The crowd was silent, but they did not move. Bundled against the cold in their cloaks, they faced the gates, gazing down the green sward of grass toward the garrison, black and ominous in the gathering light. Beyond those gates was the prison where their loved ones were being held.

Wil had been worried that they would be ordered to disperse, but Obi-Wan had guessed correctly that the Imperial officers would want every Ussan to see the extent of their ruthlessness. They would pretend to release the prisoners, but once they had Ferus, they would catch them in the net of stormtroopers ringing the Commons. He was sure of it. His job was to time his rescue of Ferus perfectly. If the people of Ussa followed through, he would have a clear shot.

Mist rose from the grass. The sky was dark gray, but the shadows were beginning to lighten as a sudden hush came over the crowd. Ferus walked slowly through the streets, and they parted before him.

He walked down the long grassy lawn alone, a tall figure in a brown traveling cloak. He stopped at the gates of the garrison.

The silence grew until not even a cough, a footstep, could be heard. Not even an indrawn breath.

The gates slowly opened. A man appeared on the steps, wearing his bright yellow prison uniform. Another appeared. Then a woman. And then they all streamed out into the Commons. A squad of stormtroopers walked alongside them, keeping them together.

The prisoners milled in the grassy square, confused, fear on their faces. They searched the crowd anxiously for the familiar faces of family and friends.

Malorum appeared on the steps. He spoke, and

his voice was amplified so that every citizen could hear it. "We are grateful to the citizens of Ussa for their cooperation in handing over the criminal Ferus Olin —"

A murmur rose from the crowd. Handing over! They did not hand him over! He came of his own free will.

A squad of stormtroopers surrounded Ferus, their blaster rifles trained on him.

"Unfortunately, because of the unruly crowd, we will release the prisoners one by one to their families, but only after they undergo additional security checks —"

A moan grew from the crowd and gathered in intensity. Someone shouted "No!" So close to freedom, the prisoners began to move forward. Nothing lay between them and the streets filled with their families.

"No," Obi-Wan whispered. "Don't move. Not yet . . ."

"The prisoners are rioting! Seize them!" Malorum called.

Here it is, Obi-Wan thought. *The double cross.* He shot up into the sky in the airspeeder, but he kept it hovering. If he went too soon, the stormtroopers would turn on the prisoners. It was agonizing, but he had to wait a few more seconds.

The people of Ussa shouted in protest, and began to move toward the prisoners. The storm-troopers raised their force pikes.

His hands tightened on the airspeeder's controls. He had to wait until the stormtroopers were distracted. If they thought he was coming in to attack, they would open fire.

The people of Ussa threw off their cloaks.

They rushed forward in a wave. The stormtroopers were overwhelmed. And confused — suddenly there were uniforms everywhere. A vast sea of yellow prisoner uniforms, but also Imperial officers, here and there. They could not fire their blasters or use their force pikes if there was a chance Imperial officers could be in the crowd.

Obi-Wan shot forward as the citizens flowed onto the Commons. They mingled with the prisoners, enfolding them until in a matter of seconds it was impossible to tell who had been a prisoner and who had not. And there were hundreds more behind them, all in uniforms, all massed in the streets, pouring out of doorways.

Trever had stolen the uniforms Mariana collected to launder, and even the material the prudent tailor had stockpiled. Working all night, each citizen had either found or fashioned a uniform until the entire city was ready to meet the Imperials.

The idea of a prisoner became meaningless. Every citizen in Ussa was a prisoner. And what Obi-Wan had counted on had happened — Malorum could not give an order to shoot, because he could not — not yet, anyway — mow down the citizens of an entire city.

Soaring above, Obi-Wan thought he had never seen such courage. Every citizen was willing to give his or her life. Everyone was committed.

Malorum, he could see, was furious — and frustrated. With a crisp order, he turned, and the stormtroopers surrounding Ferus suddenly clamped stun cuffs on him and pulled him toward the doorway.

No! Obi-Wan exclaimed in his mind. If they moved Ferus inside that garrison, he would never come out again. He was too dangerous to allow to live.

They had been taking a chance, of course. They had counted on the diversion to ensure that Obi-Wan would be able to get to Ferus in time. But Malorum's words had enflamed the crowd, and they had surged forward a few crucial seconds ahead of time. Obi-Wan was still too far away.

The garrison doors were closing. Obi-Wan would not let it end this way. He would not lose Ferus. Not like this.

CHAPTER EIGHTEEN

Obi-Wan flipped the airspeeder sideways and dived down, aiming it directly at the closing gap at the garrison front doors. He heard the screech of metal as he squeezed into the gap, and he heard a *clunk* as something on the side of the speeder was sheared off. He just hoped it wasn't something crucial; he didn't have time to look.

Ferus was being borne away down a wide hallway, surrounded by stormtroopers. Fortunately, the ceiling here was very high to allow transports and machinery through. With the stun cuffs binding his wrists, if he made a wrong move they could send a charge that would bring him to his knees. He had felt Obi-Wan, although the stormtroopers hadn't seen him, not yet. Obi-Wan felt a surge of the Force as Ferus sent it flying toward him.

Malorum happened to turn. He was dressed in a

hooded robe, as always, and Obi-Wan could only see dark holes for eyes, the dead black of hate.

He drew his lightsaber. He had no choice. Now Malorum would know for sure, if Fett had not told him yet, that a Jedi was still alive. He did not like to expose himself this way.

But Obi-Wan knew he had to do it. It was beings like Ferus who would pave the way, who would keep fighting, who would weaken the Empire in a thousand small ways that would add up to eventual victory. Now he understood Qui-Gon's words. He had seen firsthand the loyalty Ferus could inspire.

As the airspeeder descended, he slashed at the stun cuffs. He felt the shock all the way up his shoulder as the charge rang through him, but the stun cuffs clattered to the floor. He did not flinch, did not stop. He could feel the Force moving, pulsing, and he used it to Force-push the stormtroopers away as he reached down a hand for Ferus.

Ferus grasped his hand. The Force ran through them, a chain that would not be broken.

He pulled, and Ferus came up, propelled by his own strength and by the strength of the Force. Ferus swung one leg over the airspeeder and Obi-Wan pushed the engines hard. The speeder rocketed up, wobbling a bit from the added weight of Ferus and whatever had fallen off that had compromised its balance.

The blaster fire began. Obi-Wan had to deal with the speeder. He tossed the lightsaber back to Ferus. Ferus jumped to stand on the airspeeder.

He could see, out of the corner of his eye, how fast and accurate Ferus was, deflecting blaster fire on the weaving vehicle. He kept pace with the turns, amazingly able to balance without falling off. Obi-Wan careened down the wide hallway. It was hard to negotiate such a tight space on an airspeeder, especially one that wasn't balanced, and he was afraid of knocking Ferus off.

Someone shot off a rocket. They heard the *whoosh* of air displacement.

"Left!" Ferus shouted, looking back, and Obi-Wan yanked the speeder to the left.

The targeting computer sent the rocket after them. The airspeeder did a wild dance in the air, zigzagging crazily down the hall while officers and troopers dived for cover. The rocket missed them by a millimeter and exploded against a wall, sending several stormtroopers flying. Obi-Wan felt it stir his hair. That was way too close for his comfort.

The engine began to smoke. Obi-Wan pushed it one last time, making a sudden, quick right turn into an empty hallway. The speeder made the turn but then the steering gave out. Obi-Wan and

Ferus leaped off and the airspeeder crashed into the wall.

The vehicle burst into flames. The hallway filled up with smoke. Alarms went off. Sprinklers sprayed water down on the hallway.

They had seconds. Less than seconds.

Above their heads, Obi-Wan spied an air vent. He wrenched the cover off.

Ferus needed no prompting. He hoisted himself up and swung his legs inside. Obi-Wan followed, pulling himself up and into a wide plastoid duct in the air control system. He repositioned the vent. They wouldn't take long to figure out where they'd gone, but this should buy a few minutes.

Ferus began to crawl down the duct, moving as silently as a Jedi.

They had only crawled a few meters when they heard the blaster fire riddle the vent cover. They heard the clang as it fell.

They hadn't bought minutes, after all. Only a few seconds. Which, considering that they were in the midst of an Imperial garrison, wasn't nearly enough.

They quickly scurried around a curve. Ferus pointed to a filtering screen. Obi-Wan nodded. Carefully, Ferus lifted it off and disappeared through the hole. Obi-Wan followed. Ferus was balanced on a water pipe, holding the screen. Obi-Wan hoisted himself out, and Ferus replaced the screen. They were now outside the air grid and in the middle of a matrix of pipes. Some of the pipes were hot, and the air felt close and steamy.

They would have to move by hanging onto the pipes. It would take extraordinary stamina, but the stormtroopers would not think of checking for them there.

Ferus moved hand over hand quickly. Obi-Wan followed. They moved swiftly through the building until they could not hear their pursuers in the adjacent airflow ducts.

Ferus hauled himself up and straddled a pipe. Obi-Wan did the same. Ferus's forehead was damp with sweat. "Any ideas on where to go next?"

"We'll never get out of here if we don't know where we are," Obi-Wan said. "We have to find an exit."

"If we find an empty office with a datapad, we can look up the building diagrams," Ferus said. "We need a couple of exit strategies."

"Let's try it," Obi-Wan agreed.

They continued on until they found a utility panel below them. Obi-Wan hung by his knees. He closed his eyes, listening, searching for the living Force. When he was sure, he pried off the panel. Past the sensor suite inside, he could look down into an empty office. There was just enough room to crawl through.

Carefully Obi-Wan wiggled into the sensor suite and then dropped into the room. Ferus followed. The room held only a table made out of one slab of polished stone and one chair. A cloak with a deep hood was thrown over the chair. It was the darkest of maroons, the red of a terrible bruise.

"I have a bad feeling about this," Obi-Wan said. "I think we've landed in Malorum's private office."

Ferus's eyes gleamed. "We get lucky at last."

"My point is, hurry up."

Ferus moved immediately to the datapad on the table. Obi-Wan stood guard at the door.

"Find the building schematic first," Obi-Wan said. "If we don't get out of here, we can't do much of anything."

"Right. I'll download the building diagrams." Ferus quickly accessed the file and downloaded it into his pocket datapad. He tossed it to Obi-Wan while he accessed the files.

"He's got tons of surveillance files, but not much on Bellassa . . . hey, have you ever heard of a place called Polis Massa?"

Obi-Wan felt himself turn to ice. "Yes."

Ferus began to scroll through the file. "It's got about ten levels of security on the file. Must be something."

"Try to crack it."

"Okay . . ." Ferus's fingers flew over the keys. "I

got the first one . . . he hired an investigator to examine med records from the clinic. But there's no record of what he was looking for. Or if he found anything."

Obi-Wan closed his eyes briefly. Polis Massa was where they had taken Padmé to deliver her children in safety. In what he had thought was safety. It was where she had died.

Here it was. Here was the connection he was looking for. Ferus was the key, because the man who was looking for Ferus was looking for information on Padmé's death as well. The rumor was that she'd been killed by a Jedi during the "rebellion."

"He's gathering data for Lord Vader, but he hasn't transmitted any," Ferus said. "I can't make it out. The security controls are too tight."

"Someone's coming."

"Aw, I was just going to take the wheels off his chair."

"Ferus, will you come on?" Obi-Wan jumped behind the curtains. It wasn't the best hiding place, but they didn't have much choice. They didn't have time to get up into the ceiling again.

They heard the door swish open. Heavy boots thumped in.

Obi-Wan peeked through the curtain. He had to suppress a groan. It was Malorum — and Boba Fett.

CHAPTER NINETEEN

Ferus heard Malorum's voice ring through the room. He and Obi-Wan could see through a slit in the heavy curtains.

"I took a chance on you." Malorum's voice hissed like a slithering creature. "Even though you failed to bring me what I needed on Polis Massa, or Naboo. Your record, despite your youth, was impressive."

Boba Fett was no longer wearing his helmet. He stood, holding it under one arm. His dark eyes didn't flicker despite the abuse. Ferus had seen that look before, in other young beings after the wars. They had seen too much and had suffered too much at an early age. Boys like Trever. Yet Trever, despite his criminal ways, was good at heart. This one, Ferus thought, was damaged.

"You let them get away!" Malorum raised his voice and hit each word hard.

Still, Boba said nothing. Ferus was impressed and a little disconcerted at Boba's silence. The young man had a little too much assurance. It was unnerving.

Even Malorum looked unsettled. "Aren't you going to say anything? Because of you, Ferus Olin escaped and was able to return to Ussa. Now he's somewhere in this building!"

"Isn't that what you wanted?" Boba asked. "You wanted to show the citizens of Ussa that you could get him. You got him. If he's in the building, you'll find him. He can't get out."

Malorum leaned in closer. "You were hired to find him. I'm telling you that he's here. Bring him to me."

"I told you when I took the job that I needed to know everything," Boba said. "You didn't tell me Jedi would be involved."

"I didn't know."

"It was your business to know it."

"Did you recognize him?"

"No. But he's very skilled."

"Interesting," Malorum murmured. "Are you using the Jedi as an excuse for your failure?"

"No," Boba said. "It just makes the job more challenging. And more expensive."

"You have already been paid the top rate," Malorum said. "I'm not authorized to pay any more."

"Then get authorized," Boba said.

"I need you to track them right now! They could be anywhere!"

Boba still didn't answer.

"This will be your last job for me," Malorum hissed angrily. "Consider yourself authorized. Now get that lethal companion of yours and find those two. And don't fail this time."

The door opened. Boba Fett strode out. Malorum followed, the train on his robe twitching like a tail.

"That Boba seems eerily competent," Ferus murmured. "Can you imagine what his father was like?"

"All too well," Obi-Wan said, remembering a certain battle on Kamino.

Obi-Wan accessed the building diagrams and studied them quickly. "There's a landing platform next to the prison area. It's used for a service entrance and also the registration for prisoner transfer. I think we should try that one. We can get there through the piping system."

"Not to argue with you, Obi-Wan, but wouldn't you think there might be additional security in the prison?"

"Trever told me that the Imperials couldn't get the citizens of the city to help them with garbage collection, laundry, things like that — it was hard to find people who would profit from the occupation of their planet."

"Yes. It drove the Imperials crazy. They have

to import most of their support services. They hate that."

"They brought in droids to run all the internal waste removal and laundry collection systems. According to Trever, Mariana picks up the laundry from the droids at nine every morning. That means the droids have to access the service door . . ."

". . . to the landing platform, where there might be a vehicle for us to liberate. That's in about six minutes." Ferus pushed his hands through his hair. "Are you telling me that in order to get out of here, I have to break *into* prison?"

Obi-Wan nodded.

"I like your thinking, Master Kenobi."

Back up into the vent again, they squeezed along the tiny opening that led to the pipes. There was a larger outflow pipe here that they were able to crawl on top of. Obi-Wan had memorized the route, and he led the way to the prison.

Suddenly he stopped. "We must be entering the prison now," he said. "There's a security system up ahead."

"Can you tell what kind?"

"Infrared. It scans for all known body temperatures and bypasses mechanical heating systems. Just in case one of the prisoners decides to crawl up into a vent to hide, I suppose. An alarm will go off."

"Let me disable it."

"No, that will just tip them off. We're going to have to use the Force to slow our body processes down. We don't have far to go. Do you think you could manage it?"

Ferus hesitated. "Maybe. But if I can't, you'll be caught. I'm still rusty, and if I fail, we both fail. You go, Obi-Wan. I'll find another way."

Obi-Wan held his gaze. "You can do it. I've felt it. I know you can do it. I know you can be a Jedi again."

Ferus swallowed. What if he was responsible for Obi-Wan being captured? He had dragged him into this.

Come on, Ferus, I can see you thinking. Siri's crooked grin rose in his mind. *Looks like it might hurt, thinking that hard. Let's just go ahead and do it. Let your thoughts be actions until you aren't thinking at all. Just moving.*

"Let's do it," he said.

They reached out for the Force together, and he felt it grow.

I know you can be a Jedi again.

He closed his eyes, calling on the Force and willing his body temperature to drop. He felt his skin, and it was cold.

Obi-Wan began to move. Ferus followed. They moved quickly, their bodies staying cool despite the heat coming from the pipes. Ferus didn't feel it. He felt only the Force, and the connection to Obi-Wan.

Remembering the diagram, Obi-Wan kicked through a vent and they landed in a closet. They peeked out the door. They saw a droid with a repulsorlift cart filled with laundry. He stopped outside a room and entered, leaving the cart outside.

Ferus and Obi-Wan slipped out the door and leaped into the cart, burrowing underneath sheets and comforters. A moment later a load of towels was dropped on their heads. The cart lurched forward.

The cart moved slowly down the hall as the droid stopped every few meters to collect more laundry. At last they drew up in front of the door leading to the private landing platform.

The droid moved forward to access the control panel.

Suddenly there was the sound of booted feet striking the hard floor. A voice rang out: "Stop!" It was a lower-ranked Imperial officer, accompanied by a lone stormtrooper.

The droid turned. "Access to landing platform daily at this time."

"We're on high alert. No exits. That includes building utility servicing."

The sensor light flashed.

"Laundry service requesting delivery," the droid said.

"Tell them to go away," the officer said curtly.

The droid moved forward and pressed a button

on the security panel. "No laundry service today. No admittance to landing platform."

"Aw, c'mon, chief!"

Ferus and Obi-Wan exchanged a glance. It was Trever.

"Not a chief, a service droid. No admittance," the droid repeated.

"I'm not leaving."

The Imperial officer strode forward. "Then we'll blast you out. Get moving." He pressed a button, and a vidscreen was suddenly filled with Trever's image.

"Look, I've got General Malorum's robes here —" Trever said.

"He's not a general, he's Inquisitor Malorum."

"Whatever. I've got his robes, and he specifically requested this morning delivery."

"We're on high alert . . ."

"Yeah, yeah, I heard that. So you tell him he won't get his stuff. Have you ever told him one of his orders wasn't followed?" Trever shrugged. "Better you than me."

"Hold on."

Obi-Wan could see a trickle of sweat bead on the officer's hairline and drip down the side of his face. He could refuse the delivery, and Malorum would blame him. Or he could just let the delivery pass through, and Malorum would get his robes.

"Just this one delivery," the officer told the droid as he pressed the release.

The droid activated the cart and it began to move toward the doors.

They were almost there. Almost free.

An alarm suddenly sounded, and the door stopped sliding open.

"Something overrode the door," the officer said nervously.

Ferus and Obi-Wan leaped out of the cart at the same instant. This was their only chance, and they had to take it.

The officer turned, his mouth agape, and began to fumble for his blaster. Obi-Wan leaped up and Force-pushed the officer against the wall.

The stormtrooper had his blaster out. Ferus held out a hand to Force-push him away from the door, but nothing happened.

Well, it's not like he could expect to get it right every time.

He charged forward, leading with his shoulder, and slammed into the officer, knocking him down. Obi-Wan leaped through the opening, and Ferus followed.

The gravsled was empty. Trever must have taken off on foot when the alarm sounded. Ferus saw the Firespray on one end of the platform. Another silver cruiser was near the checkpoint. As much as Ferus would have enjoyed stealing Boba Fett's, the other was closer. They raced toward it.

Blaster fire suddenly peppered the shell of the cruiser. Stormtroopers were pouring after them. Obi-Wan's lightsaber was a dancing arc of light.

Ferus jumped into the cockpit. He swung the cannons toward the line of stormtroopers and blasted away.

Obi-Wan jumped inside the cruiser. Across the hangar, a dark streak dashed. It was Boba Fett, racing for his Firespray. Ferus took off.

They shot into the sky. Below, the city of Ussa became a small blue dot. Within seconds, they had blasted out of the atmosphere and were in space.

"We have to jump to hyperspace. It's the only way we can lose Fett," Obi-Wan said.

"I know."

"As long as you remain on the planet, the Empire will use you to threaten the citizens. Once we leave, you might not be able to return for a long time. Maybe never."

Ferus gave one backward glance at Bellassa. He thought of everything he was leaving. He thought of Roan.

"I know," he said again.

CHAPTER TWENTY

Once they were in hyperspace, they didn't speak for awhile. Ferus felt an enormous pain in his heart. He was not a native Bellassan, but he had adopted that world. It was his homeworld. He had made a life there. He felt as if he had been cut in two.

Obi-Wan put in the coordinates of a spaceport that orbited a pair of dying stars called the Red Twins. The Empire's reach did not extend that far, at least in terms of constant monitoring. He ran checks on the systems, giving Ferus time to recover. Ferus had gotten to know Obi-Wan better over the space of two days than he'd known him in all his years in the Jedi Temple. He had always known that Obi-Wan had courage, but he had seen his sensitivity to emotion, too.

"What was it about Polis Massa?" Ferus asked, breaking the silence. "You looked as blue as a Twi'lek when I read the name."

Obi-Wan stared into the depths of the nav computer. The glow of the screen made him look suddenly haggard.

"I can't tell you," he said. "It concerns something . . . information I must keep to myself. If I give it away, it could endanger you, and more than you. . . . It could endanger what you believe in." Obi-Wan turned to face him. "This isn't about trust. I trust you, Ferus. But I am returning to where I make my exile. If you need me, we can figure out a way for you to call on me. You don't understand this, but I believe that the future of the galaxy lies in my ability to wait."

"All right," Ferus said. "That is your task. But mine is to locate as many Jedi as I can find. There must be others. The Force-sensitive who need help. Jedi who have gone underground. I know they're out there. I'll find them. If I can establish a safe place, we can be ready for what comes."

"Another war?"

"It is inevitable. Especially since you've told me the Emperor is a Sith."

"All the more reason to wait." Obi-Wan sighed. "But before we part, I wanted to ask you something. I always suspected that Anakin played a part in your leaving the Jedi."

"Everyone played a part," Ferus said, evading the question. "What difference does it make? They're all dead now."

He had seen how hard it was for Obi-Wan to say Anakin's name. He must miss his apprentice. Ferus wondered how Anakin had died, but he didn't want to ask. He didn't want to dredge up a painful memory for Obi-Wan.

And he didn't want to tell him the real story of his resignation from the Jedi. How he suspected that Anakin had deliberately withheld information about Tru Veld's lightsaber, knowing it would fail in battle. Because of that, Darra Thel-Tanis had died. Yet Ferus had felt responsible. He had fixed Tru's lightsaber and kept it a secret, a violation of the rules between Master and Padawan. Anakin had known it, and kept it a secret, too.

It was all so long ago. Mistakes made by boys, by Padawans with dreams of becoming great Jedi Masters.

The dreams had died. It was so hard for Ferus to accept that the Jedi Order had died, too. He would not believe it. He would not allow himself to believe it. He would scour the galaxy until he found every last one of them. His cause had been Bellassa. Now it was the survival of the galaxy itself.

"I should have realized it," Obi-Wan spoke up. Ferus realized he was still thinking about Ferus's resignation from the Order. "I should have asked more questions. Something didn't feel right at the time."

"It doesn't matter," Ferus said. "I walked away. It

was the most difficult thing I ever had to do, but in a way I'm glad it happened."

"You're still a Jedi, Ferus."

"No," Ferus said slowly. "I'm not. I can never really be a Jedi again. Not just because I left the Order." He looked back, in the direction of Bellassa. "I have attachments."

"Once there was something I wanted, something forbidden by the Jedi code," Obi-Wan said. "Qui-Gon said something to me then. He said, maybe in a different galaxy things will change. The Jedi will change. Here is the change, Ferus. And I think . . . in the new order, attachments will be a strength. Maybe this is how the galaxy will be saved. So yes, you are still a Jedi."

Suddenly, a head with spiky blue hair popped out of a storage closet. "You're a Jedi, Ferus? You monkey lizard — that's galactic!"

Ferus rose from his seat. "Trever! What are you doing here?"

Trever squeezed out of the tiny space and tumbled out onto the cockpit floor. He rose, dusting off his coveralls. "What did you expect me to do when the alarms went off? I hid."

"You knew we would be heading for this cruiser," Obi-Wan said sternly. "You could have said something before we jumped to hyperspace. Why did you stay hidden?"

"I need a vacation?" Trever said.

"Great. Enjoy the ride," Ferus said. "As soon as we land, I'm putting you on the first transport back."

"You can't," Trever said. "I was recognized at the checkpoint. They have my image in their databank. They'll throw me in prison. Probably execute me for helping you escape." He grinned at Ferus's annoyed expression. "Looks like you're stuck with me."

"How lucky can you get," Ferus said.

So, despite his best efforts to become an exile, he had managed to become a Jedi again. Obi-Wan stared down at his lightsaber. Something deep stirred in him, and for the first time in a long, long while, it wasn't pain or regret. It was purpose. He understood now, more fully than he had, that justice would rise again. He couldn't predict when or how, but he knew beings like Ferus would be a part of it. When he had told Ferus that attachments could be a source of strength, he had been speaking for himself, too. The tug that had brought him to Ferus's side had been more than a concern for Luke. It had reconnected him to something he had lost. He had spent so many months thinking of the dead. Dreaming of them. Now it was time to join the living.

That was why watching over Luke was so crucial. That was why he couldn't lose hope, couldn't falter. Everything he knew was gone, and when things changed, they would not change in the way he wanted. He would not get back all that he'd lost. He realized now how much of his bitterness had been tied up in that simple, childish wish — to have back what he'd loved.

What he loved was gone forever.

What would come he couldn't see.

What he had to do to make it happen, he would do. He would do it out of more than duty now. He would do it with his heart.

They came out of hyperspace close to their destination. The Red Twins were hidden in a dense nebula, and they had to use the nav computer to make their way. Then, suddenly, they had a visual sighting, a reddish haze that looked like one faint star.

Obi-Wan gave their position to the spaceport, and they were cleared to land. Ferus dropped the cruiser neatly into the target landing area and then manually guided it to a parking space. He stretched.

"I could use a meal and a rest," he said.

"I'm afraid you'll have to wait a bit longer for that," Obi-Wan said.

Foreboding snaked through Ferus. He followed Obi-Wan's gaze out the viewscreen to the crowded spaceport. Parked only meters away was the Firespray attack ship.

Boba Fett had found them.